THE HOTTEST STATE

THE HOTTEST STATE

ETHAN HAWKE

LITTLE, BROWN AND COMPANY
Boston   New York   Toronto   London

First Edition

The characters and events in this book are fictitious. Any similarity to
real persons, living or dead, is coincidental and not intended by the
author.

Library of Congress Cataloging-in-Publication Data
Hawke, Ethan
    The hottest state : a novel / by Ethan Hawke. — 1st ed.
        p.   cm.
    ISBN 0-316-54083-8
    I. Title.
PS3558.A8165H6   1996
813'.54 — dc20   96-14702

                    10 9 8 7 6 5 4 3 2 1
                            HAD

Published simultaneously in Canada by Little, Brown & Company
(Canada) Limited

Printed in the United States of America

OCT 1 8 1996
OCT 1 6 1996

for lynn

THE HOTTEST STATE

ONE

In my old apartment, before there was any furniture, I would sit in the window and stare out at New York City. A gigantic apartment building was the only view. I would watch the people going in and out of the building's several pairs of revolving doors. Sounds boring and often it was, eyes glazed over, more from watching my own reflection than the lives circling outside — but sometimes, usually near midnight, around the corner would come the couples, casually walking home from their dates, talking for far too long outside the building. I would sit there watching, trying not to smoke too much, awaiting my furniture, thinking, Yeah, I'm really here. If someone wants to call me, they call New York City.

I met Sarah in a bar, the Bitter End. It was August fifteenth. Looking back on it, I'd like to say that it was love at first sight, but in truth I think she was just an intriguing contrast to the two women I was dating at the time. One woman's name is so embarrassing that I'll not mention it here to save myself any credibility I might have. The other girl just plain annoyed me. I kept dating her because she had this strange power of making me feel like leaving her would be a monumental personal failure on my part ("I know you," she would say).

Sarah had just arrived from Seattle and was with some people we both knew. We had been seated next to each other by this artsy-looking friend of hers who kept insisting that he had a vagina.

"Sarah doesn't think men have vaginas," he said.

"I know I don't have one," I said.

"Yes you do."

"No, in fact, I'm pretty positive I don't."

He scowled, like I wasn't getting something, and walked away, leaving the two of us alone.

"Hi," I said. "I'm William."

She didn't say anything. She just smiled and looked down. She was quiet. Her whole body — her eyes, her breasts, her arms placed neatly in her lap — was quiet. Only her hair stood out, undisciplined curls of black that seemed to belong to someone else. Her skin was unusually white and her nose appeared to have been misplaced on her face. I guess she would be called funny-looking.

We were listening to a band that I had seen many times before and I kept talking to her, saying things like "You gotta hear this next song; this one is great." I must have said that about every song they played. I'd listen until around the end of the intro and then start up again on some monologue about what a titillating guy I was (sometimes I made myself sick), and she'd smile pleasantly, wrapping her weird hair around her ears.

"I'm totally full of shit," I said. "Don't believe a word I say.

4

I'm an actor. I just thought I should tell you that right off the bat so you don't get disappointed later. Have you ever watched *Star Trek?*"

She didn't answer.

"Well, I'm kind of like Spock . . . in that episode where he tells the replicants that everything he says is a lie, and they go, 'But if everything you say is a lie, then you're lying now, because you're telling the truth, which means you're lying now,' and then smoke starts to come out of their ears and they malfunction and he gets to escape. See, you just seem a little stiff to me, and I'm trying to make sure you're not a replicant."

"You're weird," she said.

"Yeah, yeah, I am," I said. "But you're finding yourself oddly attracted to me, aren't you?"

She looked at me.

"You have nice teeth," she said. "Nice crooked teeth."

"Thanks."

"You have the strangest energy," she said. I remember that exactly.

"Energy?" I said. "I didn't know we were going to be using words like 'energy.' And when did I put myself up for your judgment?"

"I don't know. You just seem to require a lot of attention."

"I do, huh?"

"Yeah. Are you nervous?" she asked.

"No. Why would I be nervous?"

"I don't know."

"Well, I'm not nervous," I said.

We were silent, both of us watching the band again.

"Okay, yeah," I said. "I'm nervous all the time. I don't know why."

"Me, too," she said.

I was really starting to like her. I began to basically antagonize her. She had gone to Cornell — that was good for a while. She was from Manchester, Connecticut, she read only black women authors, and she'd recently ended a three-year relationship. I was in love.

We sat there for a long while, talking over the music. I couldn't hear everything she said, but I watched her. I watched her eyes move, the way she would look at me for that beat too long, my whole body going still. She seemed slightly scared of the waitress bumping into her. Her shoulders were slumped around her breasts as she leaned forward straining to hear me. I told her I was afraid I was becoming the person I had pretended to be in high school.

When I mentioned that her friends had left, she said, "I know."

"So you like the band?" I asked. At this point, the lead singer had taken off all his clothing, with the exception of some polka-dot boxer shorts, and was dancing across the stage.

"Not really," she said.

"Then why are you still here?"

She looked away — a slight smile perhaps.

"Can I walk you home?" I asked.

We walked home through the darkness of Washington Square Park. We weren't holding hands. We were just walking, slowly, eyes glancing around, watching the city move. The police were idling their cars along the perimeter and NYU kids were drinking wine and breaking glass by the dried-out fountain. The bums were whispering from the bushes, "Coke? Smoke?"

"I'm really a Texan," I said, walking out of the shadows and into the spill of light reflected off the Washington monument. "I only spent my first five years there, but I remember it. Sometimes I want to go back and live like a real man, running errands to the lumberyard, you know, bullshitting with some guy named Jimbo. 'Sure is hot today, huh, Jim?' 'You bet,' he'd say."

I had no idea where I was going with this fantasy. I was just really enjoying talking to her.

"Then I'd come home, yell at the dogs, fix some goddamn thing that was broken, and get so hot that I'd just call it a day. I'd kick back on the front porch — no screens; I'd been saying I'd put 'em up for years. Wearing a T-shirt with Dr Pepper stains on the front, I'd light up a Marlboro, open a beer, and play the guitar, mumbling a song I only know half the words to." She was watching me and seemed interested, but mostly she was watching where we were going.

"Then out of the front door would come my wife in some faded old dress that moves real slow with the wind, you know?" Sarah nodded. "She'd sing a little under her breath, lean on one of those front-porch columns, and say, 'Boy, it was hot today.' 'You bet,' I'd answer. And I'd set that damn guitar down, step right behind her, and hold her. It'd feel nice even though we were sweaty. Then slowly, kinda by accident, we'd start to kiss."

I told her my city-inspired country dream as we continued through the park back under the shadows of the dirty Manhattan trees.

"What does your wife do?" she asked.

"What does she do?"

"Yes, what does she do while you're off gallivanting around to the lumberyard?"

". . . I don't know."

"I think you better be careful," she said, stretching her arms out and then sneaking them quickly back to her sides. "She might be having an affair with Jimbo."

"You think?" I asked.

"I'm just saying you might want to leave some room in the fantasy."

I remember getting scared right then that if I ever did have sex with her, she would probably shame my meager lovemaking skills — that hair, the perfectly overweight body, the loose-fitting green dress, the legs lovingly wrapped in matching green tights were all probably more woman than I could handle.

"What's your story, huh?" I asked. "What do you want?"

"I wish I could spend my life in my room writing songs." She said this with an air of someone who hadn't been invited to very many parties.

"Don't you kinda have to play 'em for somebody?"

"No, that's the part where you have to get all tense about what everybody thinks about you."

"You don't have to care about that," I said.

"I know, but it's easier if no one ever shows up," she said. She was speaking slowly and carefully, watching the soles of her shoes lightly press against the pavement. "Besides, I don't really know anybody."

"You can know me," I said.

"Yeah?" she asked, disbelieving.

"Yeah, I'm easy," I said.

The corners of her mouth began to sneak up into a mischievous smile. "Maybe," she said, "but I'm still not sure I want to invite you over."

A cop car rolled up behind us and announced loudly from a megaphone on top of the car, "Park's closed, kids. Time for romance at home."

I gave them a wave, a little irritated that they had referred to us as kids, but I think Sarah was embarrassed that they'd used the word "romance." She instantly marched off in front of me, out of the park's darkness and through the brightly lit arch of the Washington monument. I sometimes imagine that arch to be a direct window between New York and Paris, and if I could walk through it the right way, I'd wind up on the Champs-Elysées.

"What do you do? Like for a living or for your life or whatever?" I asked, tagging along after her into the light, and through the monument.

"Right now I have a job taking care of some children, but I'm a singer, I guess."

"No shit. You really are? You sing with a band?"

"I did in college. I stopped for a year to go to Seattle, but, yeah, that's why I came back."

"You play an instrument?"

"Not really. I mean, yeah, I play the guitar and the piano but not in front of people. I can barely get the courage up to sing. . . . Once before a piano recital in high school I broke my hand so that I wouldn't have to play."

"What do you mean you broke your hand?"

"I put my hand on a doorjamb and I had my best friend,

Gaby, slam the door. It didn't really break but it turned bright blue."

"This Gaby, she was your best friend?"

She smiled, and something about her expression made me want to laugh. Her lips were just slightly too big and too red for her face. She was daring me to like her.

"You're not serious?" I asked.

"Yes," she nodded.

I did. I liked this girl. I liked the way she walked with her knapsack on her back. She had the sexy, humble stride of an Irish farm girl. When she spoke, she always seemed about to make a gesture but stopped herself.

I was also liking myself more with her than I had liked myself in a long time. When I asked her where I was walking her, she said, "One-eleven East Tenth Street." The exact address of the building I'd spent so many hours watching from my window.

"My window looks out on your front door," I said.

When we arrived at her building, I felt like I was walking onto a stage. I pointed out my apartment. We smiled at each other awkwardly and began to play our respective parts.

I stuffed my hands in the pockets of this brown suede jacket I always wore and began talking frantically. She was goofing with the ends of her dress, shifting her feet back and forth, and starting to laugh easily. She had a wonderful laugh. Her whole voice, the way she spoke, sounded tough and earthy like some kind of beautiful unpolished wood. She was soft and hard at the same time. I didn't want her to slip away.

I reached for her hand but missed it and barely caught hold

of her sleeve. When I did that, she looked up at me, panicked, and immediately plopped herself down on the front steps. She took off her knapsack, reached in, and pulled out a book.

Oh, great, I thought.

The book was Adrienne Rich's *The Facts of a Doorframe.*

"Is Adrienne Rich black?" I asked.

She smiled. I sat down next to her and listened as she read me a few poems, something about the impossibility of men. She wiggled and scratched her nose the entire time she was reading. It was very distracting.

I began reciting a Gregory Corso poem that I knew by heart (all four pages, I might add) about love in relation to marriage: " 'Not that I am incapable of love it's just that I find love as odd as wearing shoes.' "

If I had been up above, watching from my window, I would have gone berserk pounding the walls with anticipation.

As she started reading her next poem, holding the book with two hands in her lap, having stopped playing with her nose and speaking with a quiet, confident voice, I stopped her mid-sentence with a kiss. She received the kiss with all the warmth and fire, wetness, and pure unadulterated bliss any young lover could wish for — in moments we were standing, in moments we were spinning, banging into the revolving doors — kissing, kissing, only kissing. This shy woman, with loose wicked black hair, was now in my arms and three inches off the ground. I was holding her so tight, loving her lips, her deep, red, wet lips, not realizing that I had picked her up. We had to stop for a moment to regain composure when a snooping doorman peeked out to look around.

Sarah took a step away, rewrapping her hair behind her ears, pulling her dress back down in an orderly fashion. Her hand was resting gently above her breasts as if to catch her breath. Her face had burst into a full Irish blush that matched the red of her lips.

We stopped looking at each other and stepped apart. Both of us were a little dizzy. I caught her eye. To hell with the doorman. We kissed again.

An old guy with a sly glance creaked his way past us and into the building. "Well, now," he coughed.

Sarah collected herself again, an attempt at seriousness on her face.

"Where's my book?" she asked.

"In my hand." I held out her book for her.

"You held that book while you kissed me," she said.

"Yeah. I did." We didn't say good-bye. She just reached for her book, placed it neatly inside her knapsack, and stepped inside.

Back at my window, looking out at what was now HER door, I had the profound feeling that my life had changed. I did. Like when a kid lying in bed late at night stares at his dark ceiling and figures out for the first time that he, yes, even he will die. The feeling of reading the last few words to a great novel or the final image before a fantastic movie cuts to black.

Looking back now, with furniture in my new apartment, I realize that I was right: my life had changed. Not in the way I'd thought, though. I hadn't met the woman I was to grow gray with. I was twenty years old, and by the time I was twenty-one, I'd be heartbroken. I didn't know that then. I just stared out the window, wondering which light was hers, took out a huge piece of paper, got out a black Magic Marker, and in big, bold block letters wrote "GOOD MORNING" and placed it in the window.

T W O

Whenever my mother would sit me down at our kitchen table and cry about how badly I was doing at school, I would tell her, "Hey, listen. It'll all work out, Mom. I'm gonna do great. I just don't like school, but I like life." She'd get angry and tell me that the world didn't work that way. "Well, it will for me," I'd say.

I got a scholarship to college and felt that I had been vindicated. My mother only grew more sad. She told me that I'd better be careful because I was a bullshitter and that there was no sadder creature on the planet than a handsome bullshitter, because everything came easy for them and they never did a damn thing with any of it.

I dropped out of college after about six months and moved to New York. I had been there for slightly over a year and was working pretty steadily as an actor (I paid my own rent) and could hold my head high as I pissed one day into the next. I spent most of my time with this playwright friend of mine, Decker.

Decker was tall and lanky with long, greasy, dark hair but a very handsome face. His features were sharp, and he always walked around hunched over as if he were cutting through something. He'd suffered from arthritis since he was very young, so his joints were a little extra large, and with the medication he was always taking, they seemed well oiled. He'd just kind of swing around.

He was the youngest of eight brothers, and his mother had committed suicide when he was fifteen. One day after making him breakfast, she asked him if he would play hooky to keep her company. He said that he had a big test, which wasn't true, and left her. She was very moody and sometimes gave him the creeps. He hurried home from school that day, nervous for some unknown reason, and found his mother had slit her own throat.

"My mother was like a lot of good Catholics: she liked babies and blood. She just wanted to have her cake and eat it too. And, I mean, she ate it," was a joke I would often hear him say.

We'd meet sometimes at two or three o'clock in the morning at this pizza place on St. Mark's and talk until the sun came up. He was the smartest person I'd ever met. He gave me all kinds of books. I'd read them as quickly as possible, to get a chance to talk with him about them before he lost interest.

We met when I was in a play he wrote called *The Poem Is You*, about a bunch of brothers hanging out the day of their mother's wake. Being able to be in his play was one of the few things I'd ever enjoyed about acting.

The two of us had taken the entire month of June and driven across the country in what we called "a tireless venture to liberate the toll booth attendants of America." When Decker was a kid his sole ambition was to be a toll booth attendant — he thought they got to keep the money.

He was researching suicide after his mother's death and discovered that toll booth attendants had the second-highest rate of suicide next to dentists. While he still felt no real empathy for dentists, he felt a disturbingly close bond with all those tortured attendants. So every time we would come in contact with one, we would greet him or her with a demented sense of enthusiasm.

"Hey, how ya doin' today?" he asked some overweight attendant in upstate New York.

"Fine."

"Feelin' pretty good?"

"Fine. It's a dollar-twenty-five, please."

"Oh, yeah, sure. Listen — how much farther to Niagara Falls?"

"Hundred miles, about," the guy said, waiting for his money.

"Falls must be nice?" I chimed in.

"At night they're okay," he said, " 'cause they got a bunch of lights, you know? But in the day it's just a shitload of water."

"You're not depressed, are you?" Decker asked.

"You two a couple a jokers or what?"

We drove all the way across the country and back without staying anywhere more than one night. Decker didn't drive. He didn't even have a license. He did his share of the work by talking uncontrollably.

Driving toward Chicago, with a flashlight tied to the rearview mirror, and his long skinny legs and knobby knees jammed into the dashboard, Decker read the entirety of *Henry V* with a ferocious passion all through the night. The following morning his voice was beat up badly from screaming over the hum of our '83 Toyota. In Chicago Decker decided he wanted to visit his mother's grave, something that he'd never done. He was going to write her a letter and leave it by her grave site. As we tried to find the town just outside Chicago where he grew up, we quietly nursed a bottle of Wild Turkey, and Decker composed his mother's letter. He wrote several different versions, reading them over to me in his raspy Shakespeare-shot voice, asking me which I preferred. Mainly they were just lists of the things he'd been doing, telling her of girls he'd liked, introducing me, asking her if she'd seen the play he'd written and telling her how he felt like she had. I told him all the versions sounded good to me. When we were getting close, he got it in his head that the letter had to be typed.

"My mother's a real stickler for neatness," he laughed.

We went to a pawnshop and I tried to charm the lady who owned the place with small talk regarding the whereabouts of the cemetery and where a good pool hall might be. Decker sat in the back by an old manual typewriter that was for sale and quickly typed his letter.

We pulled into the cemetery parking lot, and Decker decided he couldn't go through with it. He said that I should just run over and drop off the letter. I told him that he had to do it or he'd regret it as soon as we left. He insisted and finally I agreed.

It took me close to an hour to find her grave, as the Illinois wind was blowing in my eyes so hard it made it nearly impossible to read the names. When I found it, I saw there was a small, glass-encased picture of her set into the headstone. She was beautiful. She had a round, young face. The stone said "Mother, Sister, Wife, and Friend." I wanted to leave the letter and get the hell out of there, but with the wind the way it was, I knew if I set it down, it would just blow straight away. I got down on my knees, leaning in against the wind, and began lightly digging with my hands. I was terrified she might reach up out of the earth, demanding her son, but I just wanted to dig enough to kind of plant the letter so it wouldn't blow away.

When I had neatly tucked the letter under a tuft of grass I sat there for a moment feeling a little drunk, either from the Wild Turkey or the fear. Still on my knees, with the wind whipping my hair across my face, I realized I had made my first friend. I'd done some whacked-out shit before but I'd never done it for anybody else.

When I got back into the car Decker didn't ask me what had taken so long or what I had done about the wind. He just sat there silent as we drove away. A few miles past the Illinois state line Decker started talking about what an underrated band AC/DC was.

Back in New York that summer I auditioned for and got this small part in a low-budget movie that shot in Paris. France sounded cool.

When I met Sarah I'd been roaming around the city, drinking a lot, waiting to leave. The last girl I'd slept with I'd met in a bar in the East Village, the Cherry Tavern or something. It was a tiny place with lots of wood and smoke. I'd slipped away from Decker and a whole slew of his friends only to wind up there drinking by myself. There was a little pool table in the back, and after a few minutes this girl in a tight, black miniskirt with her T-shirt tucked up between her breasts walked over and asked me if I would be her partner. We played a couple of games, our hands brushing against each other a little too often. I started helping with her shots, my hand placed around her naked waist and her ass rubbing against my thigh. Eventually she walked over to the stool I was sitting on, leaned over right in my face, and whispered, "I'd like to fuck your brains out." I was probably too drunk to register the shock I felt but I went home with her.

We were making out all the way up her stairs, so as soon as we got inside her apartment, we just started screwing. She stopped me at one point, got up naked, and walked to the bathroom and started to vomit. She couldn't have been more than nineteen. I was sure she was younger than I was.

Sarah had just moved into the city and was temporarily living with some friends across the street until the lease on her new apartment opened up. She was performing the very next night after we first met, in the same bar, the Bitter End. I took Decker along with me to check her out. He looked like a heroin addict that night. His hair was dripping with grease and his long, skinny body was all drawn out from lack of sleep. When we walked in, the place was packed with people, all of whom seemed to know each other.

I saw Sarah. She was standing to the side of the stage, fiddling with some cables and a speaker as she tried to hold a conversation with two other girls. The wires were tangled around her feet and she was tripping all over herself.

"That's her," I pointed out to Decker.

"Which one?" he asked.

I remember being shocked when he asked me that. Which one? I thought. How could he not know?

"The girl right there, playing with those cables."

"Yeah," he said. "Cute." He wasn't paying attention at all.

"What do you think?" he said. "You think this thing's gonna go on for a long time? I mean, do you think I should call up some other ladies?"

I was watching Sarah try desperately to pretend that she was interested in what the two girls were saying.

"What's with her hair?" Decker asked.

"I know. It's fucked up, isn't it?" I said, grinning.

I walked over to her. Decker fought his way through the room to the bar. I was pretty sure Sarah knew I was there before she actually turned to me.

"Hi," she said.

"Nice to see you," I said. "What's your name again?"

"You don't remember my name?"

"I'm kidding."

She didn't smile. We were silent, studying each other. With the cables still tangled in her hands, she was looking at me as if I'd caught her stealing.

"That's not funny," she said. "I'm a little nervous."

I could tell. She was standing absolutely still, her eyes darting around at all the other people. "How did you find out we were performing?"

"Some people told me."

"They did? Why?" She was a little short of breath.

"Because I asked about you."

"You did? Why?"

" 'Cause I was maybe hoping to see you again." I paused, her eyes fixed on me. I patted my pockets to see where my cigarettes were.

"You look really nice," she said with no expression on her face. "I didn't know you wore glasses."

"Well, I wasn't wearing them last night."

She took a long pause.

"Could you tell what I looked like?" she asked.

"Sometimes I wear contacts."

"Oh," she said. "How do I look now?" She dropped the cables and stood up tall, with her arms at her sides. I looked at her. She was wearing a dark green, full-length skirt and a thick, gray cotton T-shirt with a small image of the Soviet flag above her left breast. Her head was cocked slightly to the left. She was nibbling on her bottom lip. Her eyebrows were furry and unkempt. Her forehead was wrinkled in apology, but her eyes stole all the focus. I could tell they were green even in the dim light of the bar. She was definitely the most striking woman I had ever seen. Later, I'd often tell her that, because it was true. Right then I could only say, "You look good."

"I feel ugly," she said, still with no expression on her face. "And my microphone isn't working."

"You don't look ugly." I bent down to take a look at the microphone wires. She knelt next to me, her face and breath right next to mine.

"Hi," she said.

"Hi," I answered.

I arched my neck around, showing her the hickey she had given me the night before.

"Oh, my God," she screamed, a little more loudly than she would've liked to, covering the hickey with her hands. "Did I do that?" she whispered.

"Yeah." Her hands felt soft against my neck. I wanted to kiss her and tell her to please not be nervous, that I was sure she'd be great.

"Are you mad?" she asked.

"No."

She started skittishly inspecting the hickey, as if she were scared of it.

"Do you do that all the time?" she said, both of us still hunched over on the floor by the stage. People continued to crowd into the bar.

"Do what?"

"Kiss girls?"

I didn't know how to answer that.

"Oh, never mind," she said. "Of course you do."

I just looked at her, unable to say anything.

This tall, skinny black guy with a big top hat came over and said, "Hey, Sarah. I think we'll start in about ten minutes. That sound all right?"

"Fine," she said and leapt up, taking long strides fast through the crowd toward the bathroom.

"Is she all right?" he asked.

"Yeah. I think something's wrong with her microphone."

"Tell her I'll take care of it."

"Thanks," I said and followed after her.

I waited for her outside the bathroom door. The door had a little stick figure with a dress on it. I felt kind of like a stick figure with pants on. I didn't know her well enough to just go charging in there, but I definitely kind of wanted to. When a woman walked out, I held the door open with my foot and gently called out her name.

"Sarah? Ah . . . hey. That guy said he was gonna take care of the microphone business."

Then I heard her softly whisper, "Come here."

"What?" I asked.

"Come here," she said again in a quiet, rushed voice.

I carefully walked into the women's room. I saw myself in

the mirror and immediately didn't want to be there. I heard her voice again. She whispered, "Come here." The door to the first stall peeked open. I walked in and closed it behind us. She was pale. The room was bright. We were looking at one another in the fluorescent light, standing exactly next to each other. We couldn't have been closer. Her back was to the toilet and mine was next to the stall door. I think we both felt a little silly.

"I'm behaving ridiculously," she said, as if she were scolding someone else.

"Yeah," I answered. We were silent.

"Can I borrow your jacket?" she asked.

"Sure," I said, struggling to take it off in such a tight space. It was my brown suede jacket that I always wore, no matter how hot the weather. I was the type of five-year-old kid that would wear a jeans jacket in hundred-degree Texas heat because I thought it looked cool. For some reason, I was happy to give it to her. She took it in her hands.

"I'm sorry about the hickey thing," she said again, looking up at me, her face directly under mine. Her breath was cool against my face. I wanted to kiss her but I was apprehensive.

"It's absolutely all right," I said.

"Okay, you should probably go now."

"Sure," I said. I had no idea what I was doing there in the first place. I started to try to turn around and figure out how to get out of there, when she called, "Hey."

I turned back and looked at her.

"Well, . . . uh . . . ," she stammered, looking at the floor. I reached my hand out and placed it under her chin, meaning to give her a quick good-luck kiss, but as soon as our lips touched, she reached up into me hard, kissing me deeply. My jacket was still in her hands, her face stretched up to mine. I banged my leg into the toilet paper dispenser and we knocked against the sides of the stall. Her wet lips were hot against the cool of her mouth.

She stopped and used my jacket to push her hair out of her eyes.

"You really should probably go," she said, touching her lips with the back of her hand.

"Good luck," I said.

"Thank you," she said, trying to smile at me. I opened the door of the stall, turned around again, and said, "Just pretend you're someone else."

"What do you mean?" she asked, her voice slipping up a little higher.

"Just think of your favorite singer. Pretend to be her for a little while, and then you'll probably realize you're just being yourself."

"I don't think so," she said.

"Well, try to have some fun anyway," I said and walked out. When I was back by the bar standing next to Decker, I looked down and noticed my hands were shaking.

She stood there centerstage, head hung, staring at the floor, with no guitar, just the microphone in front of her. Her fists were clenched in the sleeves of my jacket. She looked up only a moment before the song began, staring right through the entire room.

I paced behind the crowd, watching her, smoking cigarettes.

"P-L-E-A-S-E stop looking at me," her avoiding eyes seemed to beg. It was exactly how much she hated performing that made her so terrific to watch.

The band was the one that she had been with at college. "Fresh from Seattle," they introduced her, "Miss Sarah Wingfield."

"That's my jacket she's wearing," I said to the guy next to me.

As the show went on, her fists unclenched from around the cuffs of my jacket and she began to complete her gestures, bringing her hands up to her chest and then throwing them back to her sides. Her soft voice was swallowing up the room completely.

When the show was over, Decker told me he wanted to cut out of there. I said I was going to stick around.

"Be careful," he said.

"What d'you mean?" I asked.

"I don't know," he said. "There's a lot of corny people in here," he added and left.

I slipped behind the stage, and in front of a whole mass of people congregating around the band, I snuck a note to Sarah written in a waitress's red ink: "YOU ARE SO FUCKING BEAUTIFUL." She bit her lip and looked away, but she was smiling.

I milled around for a couple of hours, drinking with Sarah and all her Cornell friends. We found a dark corner in the equipment room to kiss again. She was quite clear that there would be no making out where people could see us.

"Did you think I was good tonight?" she asked.

"I thought you were pretty good."

"Pretty good?"

"You were great."

"Really?"

I burst out laughing. "Yeah," I said. "You know, for a white girl."

"I was pretty good," she said.

It was hard to see her in the darkness of the room we were hiding in, but I could tell she was dreaming, replaying her performance in her head and laughing. I hadn't ever seen her take pleasure in herself, and it was very flattering.

"I like you," she said. "You're a nice boy."

"Oh, yeah? Thanks. You're a nice girl."

"See, I can be like you," she said, striking an arrogant pose.

"What do you mean?"

"I don't know. I'm tough when I sing, and my teeth get all crazy crooked like yours. That's what I feel like." She brought her fists up like a prizefighter.

"So maybe if you're so tough and mean, you should give me back my jacket?"

"No, it's mine," she said, and turned around and ran out of the equipment room.

I could barely sleep that night, imagining what it'd be like to watch her do all the things she might do to get ready for bed.

The next afternoon I asked her to the movies. We took the number 1 train to Lincoln Center. We rode uptown sitting across from one another. She was reading the advertisements above my head and I was looking at her.

"I have to leave in a month, you know," I said.

"You do? Why?"

"I'm, uh, I'm gonna be in a movie."

"Really? How long will you be gone for?"

"Just a few weeks."

"Oh. . . . You're really an actor?"

"Yeah."

"Do you like it?"

"It's the only thing I've ever been good at."

She was silent for a long time, playing with a silver heart she had hanging from her necklace, staring at it.

"Where are you going?" she asked.

"Paris," I said. The subway stopped and a few people shuffled onto our train. I stood up, walked across the floor, and sat down right beside her. Sarah started speaking more softly, playing with the threads fraying off my jeans.

"That sounds like fun, I guess," she said.

"You wanna get married?" I asked. It just came out of my mouth.

"What? You and me? No."

"I'm just kidding," I said.

"Be careful," she said, the subway lightly shaking us along.

"What do you mean?"

"Just don't say anything that isn't true. Believe me, you don't have to," she said, looking up at me.

"I won't."

"I'm kind of fragile, I think." She started picking an eyelash off my face.

"Okay," I said.

"And you scare me."

"Why?"

"Oh, please," she said, taking the eyelash on her finger and, not knowing what else to do with it, carefully placing it on her tongue.

"I didn't think I was going to feel this way again," she said. "How do you feel?" I asked.

A slight smile.

"Terrified," she said, picking up her feet and placing them under herself, sitting Indian-style on the subway's red plastic bench. "Just make sure you don't promise anything that's not a promise."

I almost said "I promise" but thought better of it. I decided to wait until I was sure that she would believe me. I already completely believed myself.

The subway stopped again.

"I don't think I can do this," she laughed.

"Do what?"

"This whole thing. Meeting somebody, liking them. It's just all so . . . I don't know. I just got here," she said. "I'll probably run away and hurt you." She was playing with my jeans again.

"You can't hurt me. Trust me. I'm serious. That's part of the problem." I tried to appear calm. I wouldn't ask for anything. I was completely self-sufficient. All she had to do was stick around and hear the jokes.

I had spent my life unable to care about things that I wanted to care about. I'd been the father of two abortions, both with my first girlfriend, Samantha. We were a terribly fertile couple. The first pregnancy occurred the first time either one of us ever had sex. Samantha didn't inform me she was pregnant until ten minutes after the abortion. I told her I would've married her, but I don't know; we were only sixteen. The second time Samantha got pregnant was a year later, right before we each went off to college. I just sent her seven hundred and fifty bucks.

When Sarah and I stepped off the subway, we ran over to and up the escalator into the Lincoln Center movie theater. It was showing a revival of *King of Hearts*. I sat through the entire movie noticing what jokes she liked. Sarah just watched the screen, while I glanced around, playing with the silver heart of her necklace and trying to kiss her ear.

"Hey, buster," she kept saying. "Watch the movie."

I told Sarah that my parents had married when my mother was sixteen and divorced by the time she was nineteen.

I told Sarah that when I was a kid my mother used to rub my back every night before I went to bed. One evening, when I was about twelve or thirteen, my mother stopped and said, "You know, William, I can't do this anymore."

"What do you mean?"

"I can't rub your back like this anymore."

"Why not?"

"Well, because you like it too much. . . . You're the type of boy who gets girls pregnant."

I had no idea what she was talking about, but she didn't rub my back anymore.

I told Sarah about Samantha and of our two abortions, proving my mother absolutely right.

I told Sarah every damn thing I could think of.

She was more quiet, more reserved with her information. She was always very deliberate about the words she spoke, unless she was sleepy. Then she would chatter on endlessly. She told me of Finnegan, her dog, the magical Finnegan, conqueror of all childhood fears. She told me stories of her year in Seattle, alone, too shy to even speak to the good-looking guy who, every day at 12:20, would come in to buy a turkey sandwich to go. "I like turkey sandwiches," I felt like screaming.

On Saturday, our fourth day together, we walked over to the Central Park Zoo and watched Gus, the polar bear, swim never-ending laps in his tiny synthetic pool.

"He's got such a pleasant expression on his face, it doesn't make you sad," she said. "You know, that he's such a big guy trapped in such a small space." We stood next to each other and watched him swim around his tank, climb out, shake himself off, and then jump back in and do it all over again. When it started to rain, we didn't run; we just strolled along right through it, straight down Fifth Avenue.

"You know what I'm gonna do?" I said.

"What?"

"I'm gonna buy a car, an old one with a big dashboard, and drive you down to Nashville. Take you to the Grand Ole Opry and make you a big star."

"Yeah? You think so?"

"We'll live off Wolf's chili and Tang. I'll walk into the radio stations and demand that they listen to you sing. They'll think I'm nuts, but then you'll walk in, wearing some outfit we stole — the best one at Woolworth's."

"Woolworth's?"

"Yeah, times'll be tough."

We were getting very wet. Her T-shirt was soaked, outlining her breasts. I started running and sliding on the wet pavement. I had on these old, beat-up shoes with barely any sole left. They were great for sliding.

"Watch out for the traffic," she yelled. She had taken off her shoes and was holding one in each hand. She walked barefoot through the puddles, with her dippy knapsack still on her back.

"Can I sing Johnny Cash songs?" she said, following me.

"Are you kidding? They eat up Johnny Cash down there."

"I don't wanna be too big a star though, okay?"

"No, not too big — just right."

She ran and tried to slide into me but with her bare feet she kind of tripped. I grabbed her and kissed her.

"I want you to move in with me." These things just kept coming out of my mouth. "I mean, you know, at least until your lease starts."

Water was dripping off her curls, weighing down her hair, making her face all eyes.

"I have a scar right here." She pointed to her stomach just below her belly button. Her wet dress stuck to the skin of her stomach, where her finger was pointing. She was sexy. Her thighs, her hips, her slight shoulders, all of them were just dripping.

"That's okay," I said. "That's okay. I don't mind scars."

"Then, yes, I'd love to move in," she said. "I mean, stay with you until my apartment's ready."

"All right then. It's settled," I said.

"Yes," she nodded, with raindrops dripping off her nose.

I thought about planting a big, sloppy kiss on her, but instead I ran ahead and did a huge slide through a puddle. When I turned around she was holding her arms up in the rain, letting the water wash all over her, around her breasts, into her mouth, and running down off her uncurled hair.

It was Wednesday night when we met, Saturday afternoon when I asked her if she wanted to move in, and by Sunday there were flowers in my apartment and female voices coming out of my stereo. I loved it.

I don't remember waking up that Sunday morning — perhaps I never slept. I was just sitting up in bed watching Sarah sleep. She'd slept naked in my bed but she hadn't let me have sex with her. I didn't care. I loved watching her sleep. The light was falling through my window, all over the blue sheets of my old bed, and onto her face. I lifted up the sheets and watched her breasts move with her breath. They seemed to be sleeping themselves. I hoped that she wouldn't wake up. I laid the sheet back over her, right up to her chin. I looked up and out at my room.

I thought, This must be what praying is like.

THREE

My father lived at 3119 Pecan Avenue in a small ranch-style house just east of Fort Worth, Texas. He lived with his friend "Brother" Taylor. The only thing I remember about Brother was that he often sat on our couch in his underwear with his hand caressing his hairy stomach. If asked why he didn't have any pants on, his only reply would be that his stomach hurt.

There was a gray, beat-up '64 Plymouth Barracuda in the driveway. We called it "The Wolf" because its fender was all twisted around and it looked like it had fangs. In the yard or maybe up on the roof would be our cat, Jake. Jake was tough. He had one eye. If I stepped on his foot, he would play it cool, like it didn't bother him, wait maybe half an hour, until I was relaxed watching TV or something, and run over and scratch the holy hell out of my leg. He was that kind of cat. I thought Jake was the coolest. I aspired to his toughness. My dad was cool, too. He was tall and weighed a lot. He hadn't shaved or cut his hair in three years. He told me he wasn't going to until my mother came back to him.

My mother wasn't going to come back. She was going to

come, like every other Sunday, to pick me up, but there was no way she was ever going to step foot inside that house. She had told both of us that. I loved it inside that house. All we ever ate was Tang and Wolf's chili. The only furniture was a giant, brown couch, a TV set, some lawn furniture, and a Steinway grand piano. There were other nifty little things like napkin holders with dirty limericks printed on them, hundreds of Dr Pepper cans, and fancy, old standing ashtrays. The whole place smelled of Kool cigarettes.

My favorite thing to do, besides watching old westerns with my toy guns spread out in careful preparation for the execution of bad guys, was to sit underneath my father's grand piano while he played. He knew all of Willie Nelson's *The Red-Headed Stranger* by heart, and he'd play his own rendition of the album over and over. As near as I could tell, most of the songs were about this guy, the red-headed stranger, who missed his wife so bad he killed her. All weekend long my dad would try to teach me those songs and then, come Sunday about five o'clock, he'd send me back to my mother. When my father lived on Pecan Avenue, I was five years old and he was twenty-four.

The last weekend I spent with him before my mother and I moved out of Texas, I got to the house and we immediately went out to the barbershop. He finally wanted a shave and a haircut. When it was done, I didn't recognize him and started to cry.

He carried me out to the Barracuda and we sat there. It was always hot in that car when we'd first get in. The air was still and it smelled of burning vinyl. We sat in there sweating for a long time, the sun beating through the dirty windows. My father hadn't even flipped on the ignition.

He turned to me and said, "Listen, William, your mother and you are moving away and I can't come after you. I can't because, because, uh . . . I can't. It's killing me. It's really killing me. Do you understand?"

I didn't. His face looked so different I couldn't even recognize his voice. He kept rubbing his eyes really hard — too hard, I thought.

"When I get some money together I'll try to fly you out as much as I can, but it won't be very often, okay? It won't be as often as I want, you understand? You just gotta remember this though, all right? I'm not the one leaving Texas, all right?"

"All right," I said. I really had no idea what he was talking about. I was just sweating like crazy.

"You oughta take off your jacket, William," he said. "Do you want to take off your jacket?"

FOUR

First we bought a mattress. I was very excited about that. I had high hopes for that mattress. Sarah's apartment was now available and I was helping move her in. I gladly lugged the mattress up her five-story walk-up. I wanted to get laid so badly I could barely speak to her anymore. We would fool around for hours, sometimes all night long, but we had not had sex. It seemed to me that I was being tested. I couldn't tell Decker or anyone that I wasn't getting laid. It seemed ridiculous.

Sarah's apartment had one room, with the exception of a long corridor that led to the bathroom and the front door. When I brought the mattress in, I set it down and saw Sarah sitting on the hardwood floor, barefoot in her green dress. She was looking around at the walls. I stood behind her. I tried to imagine what she was thinking. The only sound was of a warm breeze moving through the leaves outside her two little windows. It was beginning to smell like school outside. I could feel the summer ending. I knew having her own place meant a lot to Sarah. I wanted her to sit in her own apartment and just listen. I didn't want her to have to lug anything up the goddamn stairs. My only desire was to be inside her and to look into her eyes.

I ran down the stairs to get the rest of her stuff. I was beginning to get scared that maybe I was falling in love with a woman that was never going to allow herself to love me back. Sometimes I'd get angry but I'd try not to. It felt good carrying her things. It calmed me down.

One of Sarah's new neighbors dropped by and knocked on the door. She was an old Hispanic lady who'd lived in the building for thirty-seven years. She gave us some brownies wrapped in tinfoil. She said we looked like a nice couple.

When everything was out of the lobby and up in Sarah's room, I sat on her window ledge and smoked a cigarette.

"I think we should paint tonight," she said.

"Aren't you sleepy?" I said hopefully. "I'm bushed. Why don't we just have beer and maybe try out this mattress? We can paint in the morning."

"I think we should paint tonight," Sarah repeated, walking over and sitting in the other window.

"All right, sure, yeah, painting's good," I said, a little sullen.

"Well, what do you want to do?"

"You know what I wanna do. But painting sounds okay, too." I was making myself sick. I was literally sulking. I hated being inside my own body. I thought about when I was a high school freshman and how I'd be disgusted when I'd hear stories about guys who broke up with girls just because they couldn't score. I would've traded in my bike just to have a conversation with one of those girls.

I moved over and started opening up the paint cans. I picked out a roller while she followed behind me with a brush. Sarah put on an old T-shirt with French writing across it. It was red and clung tightly around her breasts, mocking me. I asked her what the words meant, and she said with a smile, "I can't get enough."

I took my shirt off. Sarah gave me two little blue Indian stripes on the side of each cheek, and I painted an oval around each of her eyes with my finger.

I'm a terrible painter. I'm very easily distracted. We hadn't been painting half an hour before she had one giant blue handprint on her ass and one directly across the French words on her left breast.

"Does that make you feel tough? Huh? Is that it?" she asked, threatening me with her brush. With the ovals around her eyes, she looked like The Madwoman of the North.

"Yeah, it does," I said.

"Well, buster, you better get serious about your painting, because we're not going to bed tonight until this entire apartment is blue."

Never has there been such an enthusiastic painter.

After the place was pretty much done, Sarah was hunched over an electrical outlet doing the final touches. She had tied her hair up in a bun. I saw one clear drop of sweat sneak down her neck and hide in her T-shirt.

I walked over to the refrigerator, took out a beer, opened it, and placed it cold against her cheek.

Sarah had a little radio that was playing a mix tape of hers. We started to dance, more just shifting our weight side to side. I spread my fingers out across her back, hoping my hand felt strong. She kissed my neck, placing all her weight on me. We danced to the entire seven minutes and two seconds of Isaac Hayes's "By the Time I Get to Phoenix." I picked her up, and carried her to our mattress.

"Don't pick me up," she said.

"Why not?"

"I don't like it."

"I do." I set her down on the bed and she moved up, placing her back against the wall.

"You shouldn't have to prove you're stronger than me," she said.

"I'm not."

"I can't pick you up, though."

"So?" I lay down exasperated across the mattress, staring up at the ceiling.

"It makes me feel weak."

"But you're not weak," I said.

"Let's get some sheets?" she said, jumping up and rummaging through one of her bags.

"Do you know how dumb I feel?" I asked.

"What do you mean?"

"Well, when you're thinking about sex twenty-four hours a day, it significantly detracts from your intelligence."

"We should have done it that first night," she said. "The first night we kissed I wanted to sleep with you. You gave me too much time to think. I didn't think you were going to like me."

"I didn't think it was gonna be a one-shot deal."

"Oh, come on," she said, bringing the sheets over and sitting on the mattress next to me.

She had turned off the lights, except for a small lamp on the floor that was casting peculiar long, misshapen shadows.

"When is it going to get ugly?" I asked, sitting up. "When's it going to turn abusive?"

"It always does," she said.

"What kind of nasty things do you think we'll say about each other when the breakup happens?" We both sat on the mattress with our backs against the wall and thought for a moment. The single lamp lit our faces but left the large, looming shadows on the wall behind us.

"That bitch," she said.

"What a liar he is," I said.

"Cold, whiny little girl."

"Egocentric bastard."

"She can't even sing."

"He calls himself an actor.

"Isn't that strange," I said. "That'll happen. I'll come in one night, it'll be late, and I'll say, 'Listen, I need to talk to you.' "

"What's going on?" she asked, affecting a pose of an estranged wife.

"I don't know. I've just been doing some thinking."

"Thinking about what?"

"Us. . . . You know what I mean. . . . I hate it that we're always fighting like this." I was kind of smiling, not sure where to go next.

"Yeah?" she said, encouraging me to continue.

"I think we need a little space is all."

"Space for what?"

"Hey, don't make this any harder than it is. It's over and we both know it," I said, staring straight into her eyes.

"Is there someone else?" she asked, getting very serious.

"I really don't want to get into this."

"Who is it?" she demanded.

"You see, I can't even talk to you anymore."

"I don't believe these words are coming out of your mouth."

"Oh, come on. Don't make this a big drama. The point is we're over and we both know it," I said.

Sarah's eyes started to water and then she burst into tears, placing her head in her hands. I just sat there mystified.

"Oh, God, I'm such a fool," she said. "I can't do this. I promised myself I wasn't going to do this."

"We were joking."

"I spent a year collecting myself in Seattle just to make sure something like this wouldn't happen."

"Nothing happened." I paused and tried to bring her hand away from her face. "Don't start having some self-fulfilling prophecy that I'm going to hurt you."

"I'm not," she said, getting irritated.

"Let me tell you something. If you could be inside my body when I see you or hear you or touch you or think that I might see you or I might touch you, you would stop crying and slap me. Because I'm either crazy about you or I'm going crazy."

"You're going crazy," she said.

"Oh, yeah? Is that what you think?"

"Yeah. That's what I think."

"Oh, yeah?" I said, imitating the voice of some oldtime movie villain and standing up.

"Yeah."

"Well, if you don't say right now, 'I'm going to get over any stupid hangups I might have and fall desperately in love,' I'm going to jump off this bed."

"I'm not going to say that," she said, still very serious.

"SAY IT," I insisted, inching my way toward the edge of the bed.

"NO, I don't have stupid hangups."

"SAY IT."

"I'm trying to talk to you."

I screamed as I jumped off the mattress, jumping high and landing low on her hardwood floor (hurting my knee, I might add).

"Are you okay?" she asked, kneeling over me, looking at me lying flat on her floor.

"Say you're falling desperately in love with me, and I will come back to life," I said.

"NO."

"Say you're falling desperately in love with me, and I'll come back to life."

"What do you mean by 'love'?"

"Ahhhh . . . I'm dying."

"You're not dying," she said.

"Say you desperately want to kiss me passionately and I will come back to life."

"I desperately want to kiss you passionately."

After a moment of kissing, she said softly, "Here, lie down." With Mad Woman ovals still painted around her eyes and her fingers covered in blue, she began to undo my belt. I knew what was happening and it was nice, but it wasn't what I wanted.

A few days later Decker had a party. It wasn't intended to be a party but that's what happened whenever I went over to Decker's place. He always invites too many people. The plan had been for Decker and his girlfriend of the moment, Kim, to join Sarah and me for a trip to the carnival. There was some kind of amusement park that Decker and I had seen over on the 42nd Street pier, and we figured that a roller coaster ride would be a good way to mark the end of summer.

Kim was from Minnesota and had fake tits. I knew she had fake tits because I slept with her first. She was so sweet all the time that she kind of made me depressed. I only went out with her a couple of evenings. She spoke in this real high, annoying, unintelligent voice, like a cartoon character.

She told me that the only time she'd met her mother was at her father's funeral. They went out for a big steak dinner in Minneapolis and had a pretty decent time, but Kim never heard from her again. Two years later, her little brother killed himself by setting himself on fire. That's when she got the fake tits and moved to New York to become an actress. When she was telling me this story I wanted to stop her; I knew I wasn't going to be nearly nice enough to warrant hearing these personal details. I only had sex with her once. She lightly patted my back the whole time, continuously whispering, "Good boy."

Decker liked her, though. He said he was experimenting with the idea of going out with someone who liked him. I asked him once whether he didn't think she was a little witless for him. He said that he didn't think anyone was stupid, that it was remarkable the kind of things some people wouldn't let themselves think.

His apartment was a dump; there was sewage coming up through the drain of his bathtub (he was a member of a gym solely for the purpose of bathing), there was a hole where a vent used to be going directly from the kitchen to the bedroom, and there were pots and pans spread out on top of bookshelves and in corners to collect dripping water.

It had roof access, though, and that was great.

His place was on 39th Street at Eighth Avenue. Sarah and I took a cab up there. Sarah had been jittery all night getting ready to go.

She stopped the cab on the way up to run into London Drugs and buy some lipstick. I sat in the cab, trying not to stare at the meter. The cabbie was a middle-aged black guy who seemed a lot more patient than I was.

"How ya doin' tonight?" I asked him, leaning up on the back of the front seat.

"Yes, I am doing very good," he said with a French-sounding accent.

"Where are you from?" I asked him.

"Haiti."

"Oh, yeah? You still got family over there?" Some people hate it, but I love bullshitting with cab drivers.

"Yes, my wife and my children are there."

"Do you ever get to see them?"

"Once a year when I am in luck. I send them money every month." His accent was fantastic.

"It's hot in Haiti, huh?" I said.

"*Oui,* very hot. Where are you from?" he asked, looking at me through the rearview mirror.

"Texas."

"It's hot in Texas, no?"

"Yeah, it is."

"Do you have family there?" he asked me.

I paused for a second. "Yes, I do," I said. We looked at each other. "But I don't send them any money."

I tried to think if I knew anyone who was actually born in Manhattan.

Sarah jumped back in the cab, I nodded at the driver, and we took off. Sarah pressed her knees up against the back of the front seat, pushed her dress up between her legs to keep it from slipping down, wiped her black hair off her face, took out a little mirror, and began tinkering with her lipstick. I could see her green eyes in the makeup mirror. I looked up and could see the cab driver's brown eyes in the rearview mirror. There was something about New York City that made me feel like a Texan and something about Sarah that made me feel like a man.

✿　✿　✿

49

The first thing that went wrong that night at Decker's apartment was that he had invited about fifteen other people. The second problem was that one of them was Samantha, my first girlfriend.

Our junior year of high school Samantha's goal had been to "take cheerleading more seriously." She was beautiful, in an obvious way, with long, blond hair, manicured eyebrows, wine-colored nails, and a near-perfect figure. She was a little short and used a lot of hairspray, a habit left over from growing up in New Jersey. The best thing about her was that she had these huge sarcastic eyes. She was now a junior at Columbia. She was actually surprisingly intelligent.

She had come for the carnival dressed exactly as a hot September evening would ask — in as little as possible.

She was sitting out on Decker's roof on the back of a plastic chair, her neck glistening and her fingers lightly scratching her naked stomach. The city looked huge behind her, with all the midtown office buildings and a flashing yellow light above the Chase Manhattan Bank alternating the time with the temperature — 8:30 and 87°.

I held Sarah's hand tight, making sure everyone knew we were a couple. She was using her other hand to try and mat down her hair.

Decker was on the roof with a green bottle of Gordon's Gin hanging from his left hand. Decker never drank beer. He was talking to Kim, trying to keep the conversation lighthearted, but she looked venomously serious.

"I'm not saying you look bad," Decker said, defending himself. "I'm just saying I wish you were wearing a dress. I find you much more attractive in a dress. I'm not saying that to be mean, but you asked. And, yes, I wish you were in a dress."

"I felt like wearing jeans tonight," she said in her high-pitched midwestern accent.

"So wear jeans." He looked over at me and smiled.

"Do you want me to go home and change?" she asked. She was wearing tight Levis and a white T-shirt with no bra. Her nipples were always hard.

Decker hesitated for a moment and said, "Yeah, I do."

"You're such an asshole," she said. "I'll be right back." She started walking off the roof, turned to me, and said, "I can't believe you're friends with him," and walked out.

"There's two things I can't believe," I said, moving across the roof next to Decker. "One is that you asked her to do that, and the other is that she's doing it." I really wanted Sarah to like Decker and I didn't think he was making a stellar first impression.

"Are we gonna go to the carnival?" I asked him.

"Yeah, I guess," he said. "We're just going to have to get everyone motivated."

"Why did you invite so many people?" I asked.

"They wanted to come," he said, grinning.

Sarah and I drifted around the party. One of Decker's friends was a dwarf who was an incredibly sweet guy but a little intimidating at first. He had ludicrously long hair that almost dragged along the floor. There were quite a few bouncy girls with blond hair and some heavy-duty pretentious guys. I felt like Sarah was my proof that I was different from everyone else. I just hoped that no one could tell we hadn't had sex yet. Decker's roommate, Samuel, was there. He had chopped purple hair and a tattoo of a rooster hanging from a noose on his arm. I didn't see too much of him. He was a recovering speed freak who had ruined many of Decker's late-night philander-ings by wailing himself to sleep.

Sarah was always painfully shy in groups, and this was a particularly creepy gang. She barely spoke while we were there. Everyone was already drunk. I wrapped my arm around her and made all the necessary introductions.

I tried to nonchalantly avoid Samantha, but at one point she situated herself directly in front of us, waiting for me to say something.

"Sarah, this is Samantha," I said. "Samantha, this is Sarah." They shook hands, both looking uncomfortable. I stood there feeling a little too tall.

"Did you ever date her?" Sarah asked me when we walked away.

"Uh, yeah, I did. I told you about her."

"Oh, Samantha," she said, probably remembering the abortions. "I didn't know she was going to be here."

"No, neither did I," I said.

Sarah felt very far away, but I thought that was all right. I did, too. I felt like maybe I'd moved on, like I was growing up. I wanted to go to the carnival soon though. I wanted to start having fun.

Decker said that he had to wait for Kim to come back. We all just stood around for half an hour, an hour maybe, drinking and laughing. I was having a good time, fantasizing that Sarah and I were Franklin and Eleanor Roosevelt at some Roaring Twenties bash.

Sarah exited to make a phone call. When she came back on the roof, she announced she was leaving.

"What do you mean? Where are you going?"

"Turns out Dave Afton is playing downtown. I should really go see his show."

"What do you mean? We're going to the carnival," I said.

"I don't want to go to the carnival."

There was a long pause.

"But we were supposed to go to the carnival," I said.

"I know, but I told you I hate those things." Sarah had one hand reached around her back grabbing a tight hold of her other arm.

"Dave wants me to sing with him maybe, so I should really go see him play."

Now, I know Dave Afton and I've seen him play a bunch of times. I refer to him usually as "the-guy-with-the-teeth." He has stupid blond hair, blue eyes, beads hanging down his neck, and these ridiculous big, phony teeth. He smokes fancy English cigarettes and sings pretty songs that girls love, but I have never known a guy to actually enjoy watching him sing. I was also convinced that this whole getting her to sing on his album bit was a scam.

"You mean the-guy-with-the-teeth?" I said.

"Yeah, him," she said. "Listen, this is a job. This is what I'm here in New York for. You don't need me here."

"All right. I'll leave with you."

"No. You go to the carnival with your friends. I'll talk to you tomorrow."

"Fine. Fuck off then," I said.

An indignant expression seized hold of her face. She grabbed her purse and tore out of there, probably thinking I had just revealed my true self. I stood out there on the roof and stared around the party. Samantha was flirting with

Samuel. Decker was acting out the entire story of a musical called *Stop the World, I Want to Get Off.* I'd seen him do it before. Everyone else was laughing.

After about half an hour of drinking, pacing, and running my hands through my hair, I left the party. Drunk.

When I arrived at the bar she was sitting alone, smoking, looking depressed. That made me happy.

"Hi," I said as I sat down next to her.

"Hello," she almost whispered.

"I'm sorry, are you?" I asked.

"What are you sorry about?" she said.

All I could think of was that I was sorry she was mad at me.

"I didn't like tonight," I said.

"Me neither," she said. We watched Dave and his teeth sing for a while.

"Why aren't you at the carnival?" she asked.

"I don't know."

"Don't tell me to fuck off," she said, looking up at me defiantly.

"Okay, I won't."

"It's not nice."

"No, it's not."

We sat some more in silence.

"Did you ever hear the one about the guy who wanted to tell a girl how much he liked her, but all he did was stammer and stare and say mean things when he meant to be funny?"

She gave me a half-cocked smile.

"Yeah, I think I have," she said.

"Uh-huh. I think you heard it tonight."

"I'm sorry, too," she admitted. "Did you ever hear the one

about the guy who brought a girl to a party where it seemed like he'd slept with just about every girl there?" she said, looking me over. I tried to smile.

We turned back toward Dave.

"Gosh, he sure is fantastic," I said in quiet, sarcastic awe.

"You're delusional."

I leaned across the table and tried to kiss her. She stopped me short and continued watching the stage.

"Why not?" I asked.

"Not here. I don't like to kiss in public."

"If you don't want to kiss me, you don't want to kiss me."

"I don't want to kiss you here."

"Well, let's get out of here then." I leaned over, pawing at her arm, sloppily trying to be sexy.

"I don't want to leave."

"Christ. What the fuck DO you want to do?"

She stared at me, an evil, malignant look, and then slowly put out her cigarette.

"Is this where it turns abusive?" she said.

I stopped. I felt myself grow still for a moment — very still and very angry. Then in one motion, I stood up, picked up my chair, and smashed it into the wall next to us. I didn't mean to. I meant just to kind of hit it or something, but it smashed to bits. The people around us turned and stared at me. I was still holding a piece of the chair, and my hand was throbbing. I watched Sarah race out of the bar.

"Please stop!" I yelled as I crossed the street after her, car lights streaking across both our faces. Adrenaline was coursing through my brain. She stopped. We were standing on a small cement island where Bowery meets Cooper Union.

"Look, I have no idea what's going on," I said, catching my

breath. "I don't like myself either. I don't know what's happening to me. I don't want to tell you to fuck off. But you gotta
understand, everything in my life feels different. I just want
so badly to know if you like me. And I know how asinine that
sounds. If you want me to leave you alone, I will, but sometimes . . . sometimes you meet somebody and you know that
whatever you did before, whatever your life was before, it
must have been right . . . nothing could've been too bad or
gone too far wrong because it led you to this person. You're
that person. Do you want me to go away?"

"No," she said.

"What do you want me to do?" I asked. We were silent. She
was looking out at the street, her eyes moving quickly around
like she was talking to herself. My body felt as if it weighed
ten million pounds.

"I'm sorry, I'm sorry," she said, taking my hand and leading
me across the street. "Don't let me do this to you." She
stopped quickly and turned around in the middle of the inter-
section.

"Why do you like me so much?" she asked, examining my
eyes.

I stood absolutely still.

"I just do."

"And you want to have sex with me?"

I nodded. It seemed like it might be a trick question.

"Don't wonder anymore if I like you, okay? I do." My
whole back relaxed. "I think you're beautiful, and I want to
have sex with you, I do. It's just —" The light changed, and
she ran across the street. I couldn't move.

"COME ON," she yelled. I could see her eyes clearly all
the way over on the sidewalk.

Cars were driving around me honking their horns. I felt the heat of a truck brush across my face. It wasn't like I wanted a car to hit me or anything. It was more like I didn't believe they were there.

Finally the light changed again and I walked over and stepped up next to her on the sidewalk. She took one of my hands with both of hers and held it tight against her dress.

"Let's go home," she said.

We messed around all night, naked on her mattress. The start of morning turned the entire apartment a dark shade of green. Sometimes for a moment maybe we fell asleep; it was hard to tell. The air was thick and smelled heavy of salt. Our bodies were wet, and I would find myself positioning us so that we could accidentally start to have sex. As things would move close, she would writhe her body around and slip away. There was something secret about her bed. Her whole body felt clean, damp, and rich, like it was far underground. The sheets were ripped from their corners, and I could feel the coarseness of the mattress under my back. She slid herself on top of me. Her heavy breasts slipped across my chest. I wanted to be inside every part of her body. She would tease us both. Finally, in complete silence, I let myself come into my hand. I didn't want her to know. After she fell asleep, I stood up and tried to keep my balance as I walked to the bathroom and washed my hands.

The next morning I woke up to the sounds of Sarah clamoring in the kitchen region of her room. She was fixing ham
and eggs for one (she was a vegetarian) and toast for both
of us.

Rolling to my left, I put on my glasses and could see Sarah
skirting around in my boxers. Her green dress lay on the floor
by our still unconsummated mattress. Everything she did, she
did with deliberate poise, but there was something uncoordi-
nated about her that was goofy. That's the part I liked.

"What's the story, morning glory?" she said, carrying our
breakfast plates over to the bed. "I'm not mad, are you?"

"No, I'm not mad," I said, slipping on my jeans.

"Good, because I have something to show you, but you
can't be mad."

"I'm not."

"Well, you can't get mad either."

"I won't."

"You promise?"

"Why am I starting to think I'm going to get mad?" I said.

She handed me a pamphlet of Xeroxed papers along with my eggs and ham. "I thought you should read these."

"What are they?" I asked, holding them in my hand, and setting the plate down.

"Read them."

Rape and the Twentieth-Century Man — four pages of tiny Xeroxed words on how many rapes per second there were across the world.

"What does this mean?" I asked her.

"Nothing. I thought you might find it interesting."

"Why would I find this interesting?"

"Because it's important."

"But why is it important right now, this morning, to me?"

"Don't get mad," she said, kneeling down on the mattress next to me.

"Did I attack you or something last night?"

"You threw a chair."

I was silent, staring at the pages.

"I did it because I like you. Does that help?"

She shook her head no.

"I'll read it later." I set the papers down beside the bed and picked up my eggs.

She got up, and casually started eating her toast by the window.

"Decker?" she said. "He's your best friend?"

"Ah . . . yeah."

"And that girl Kim?" she asked. "Are her breasts real?"

"I don't think so," I said, getting real unsure of the direction this conversation was heading.

"Do you know what it's like to wear a dress?" she asked.

"No."

"It feels very vulnerable."

"So wear pants."

"Then I feel ugly. My thighs are fat, and my breasts are too big."

"Your breasts aren't too big. They're abundant," I said, putting my jeans on. I stood up and walked over to her by the window.

"And you've got sexy thighs," I said, resting my hands on her legs. Her pale thighs were covered with thousands of tiny little pink dots.

"Have you ever tried on a dress?" she said.

"No."

"Would you?"

"No."

"Why not?"

"Sure, sure I would," I said.

"Put on my dress."

"Come on, Sarah."

"Why not? I might find you more attractive in a dress," she said with an impetuous smile.

"Put on your dress?" I asked and stepped away from her, trying to figure out how I had lost such complete and total control of my surroundings.

"Yes," she said, enjoying watching me get uncomfortable.

"All right," I said. So, shirtless, with my jeans on, I tried on her green dress, picking it up, pulling it on over my head, letting it slide over my back, cascading, floating above my knees. Sarah was getting a very perverse thrill out of watching me do this.

"Now take off your jeans," she said, perched on her windowsill.

My whole body was nervous. I took my jeans off. Sarah was wearing my underwear, so I was naked underneath her dress. I felt the easy September breeze moving through the flowers in her window and around my naked, dress-bound legs. I stood there grinning at her, still nervous, simply staring. My knees were shaking a little but I felt oddly sexy, like a dangerous man doing dangerous things — uniquely aware that I was a man. You couldn't take my manhood away with a mere dress, I thought proudly.

"Now lipstick," she said.

"NO," I said fast.

"Why not?" she asked.

I paused, thinking about it. "Because then I'd feel like a girl."

"Is there something wrong with being feminine?"

"No."

"Then put on lipstick."

"I'm not feminine," I said.

"Oh? Not even for a minute?" She was having a great time.

I walked closer to her — the woman in my underwear — seized by a strange desire to make it with her, to burst through her dress, taking her like a Scotsman (I am part Scottish).

"No, not even for a minute," I said, placing my hand on her crotch. She bent her neck into her shoulder and giggled.

I kissed her as I thought a man might (even a man in a dress), laying her down on the bed. She was rubbing my breasts, making me uncomfortable. I moved down, kissing her stomach, my hand on my underwear touching her, her hands on her dress touching me.

"Oh, jeez, what time is it?" she asked, pushing me away, reaching her head around to look at the clock.

"I don't know," I said, still mauling her.

"Oh, no, I have to be at work. It's eleven-forty."

She leapt off the bed and ran into the bathroom, quickly changed, and put two red barrettes in her hair.

"Oh, William, I forgot," she said from the doorway. "Will you come with me to my mom's this weekend?"

"Sure," I said quietly. My own death was coming. I was sure of it. I stood up and watched her exit, finding myself alone in her room, with a plate of cold uneaten ham and eggs, a green dress, an erection, and having narrowly avoided makeup.

SEVEN

I had to talk to somebody. Decker met me at Tompkins Square Park. He was pale and hungover. We each bought a large container of Gatorade, sat down against a chain-link fence, and watched a bunch of guys play basketball. For a couple seconds it looked like there would be a fight. Some frat boy with blond hair was getting all bent out of shape, trying to start something with a much smaller Hispanic-looking guy.

"Leave it to a fraternity brother to pick a fight," Decker said to me. "One of the many bona fide reasons everyone should drop out of college."

On the other side of the playground was a group of guys playing baseball. Every time one of the baseball players would get a hit, the basketball courts would scatter with people yelling "HEADS UP." Then the basketball players would toss the baseball back and start all over again. Every now and again a basketball would roll through the infield and the base-ball players seemed happy to return the favor.

It took me a while to get around to telling Decker that Sarah and I hadn't actually slept together. He and Kim had finished their night by having sex on the Staten Island ferry. No one ever went to the carnival.

"I bet this is good for you," he said after I told him the saga. "You screw around too much anyway. That's probably half the reason you're so crazy about her."

"I really thought we were going to finally sleep together this morning, you know? I mean granted, that'd be pretty sick if every time I wanted to have sex, I had to put on a dress."

"What's her deal?" he asked, staring straight out at the basketball game.

"I don't know."

"Well, trust her instincts. She's probably right. First of all, you're not exactly a piece of cake to be with."

"What d'you mean?"

"You're pretty skittish. You just don't seem like the kind of guy who would stick around."

"I don't like it when people say things like that — everyone telling you something's true about yourself so much you start believing it."

"Does she get you off at least — you know, jerk you off, give you a blow job, or something?"

I stared at him, not sure if what he had just said pissed me off or not. It was uncomfortable sitting on the pavement.

"I don't want any more blow jobs," I said, looking back out at the game.

"Someday I'm going to remind you of that comment and you're going to be deeply ashamed," he said solemnly.

"I have to stop seeing her," I said, mostly just to hear how it sounded.

"Why?" he asked. I don't think he really felt up for a conversation. His face was even paler now.

"Because . . . I'm scared out of my mind."

"Smart girls are tough. They're a pain in the ass," he said. He wasn't grasping the situation's urgency.

"There's a difference between someone who's smart and someone who doesn't like you," I said.

"I'll tell you one thing," he said. "There's a difference between a smart girl and a girl who doesn't like to give blow jobs." I ignored him. We were silent for a while.

"Sometimes I think that if I could get her to love me, then that would mean everything I don't like about myself would've disappeared."

Decker looked over at me.

"She wants me to go with her to her mom's," I said. "You think I should go?"

"Of course you're gonna go."

"What d'ya mean?"

"You're crazy about this girl. You've got no options."

EIGHT

An eerie, slow metamorphosis took place in Sarah as we traveled up to her mother's. Inside Port Authority, Sarah ignored all the bustling commuters and used her reflection on the glass of a cigarette machine to put on blazing red lipstick, a bunch of eye makeup, and a little bit of rouge. Something about Sarah in makeup made me laugh. She looked off-balance. Inside the bathroom on the bus, she changed out of her brown dress and came out in a black, floor-length skirt with a sexy, green silk top.

She also began to get increasingly worried about my clothing. I thought I looked sharp. I had on my favorite T-shirt (it was navy blue and classy-looking) and these first-rate cotton khaki pants. I'd washed my hair, put in my contacts, and was wearing my old Justin cowboy boots.

Finally, at the Machester bus station, as we waited for her mother to pick us up, Sarah put on earrings and a headband and experimented with a completely new personality. She started speaking loudly and confidently about whatever popped into her mind. She told me that she loved bus stations — they always made her feel romantic. She said it didn't bother her at all that they smelled like cigarettes and urine.

Mrs. Wingfield was sixty-seven years old. Her neck and her head were perched far forward off her shoulders, and she moved around her house in quick, fragile movements like a dying bird.

She served a tuna fish and macaroni casserole, tiny pieces of fried ham stuck through with toothpicks, and large ice-filled glasses of Crystal Light lemonade. She poured herself an equally large glass of Riunite white wine. Her face was Sarah's exactly, only thinner and hollowed.

I had never met a girl's mother so officially. My mother told me once that my father had scored big points with her mother by eating large portions of my grandmother's cooking. He ate obscene amounts of chicken-fried steak and black-eyed peas and won my mother's hand in marriage. I wasn't actively seeking a wedding or anything, but I was sure going to give that tuna casserole my best shot.

To start the meal we all sat down and held hands. Sarah and her mother bowed their heads in unison and began a prayer:

> Father, we thank thee for this food,
> and for all thy many blessings.
> Bless them to our use,
> and us to thy service,
> and make us ever mindful of the needs of others.
> Amen.

They recited this with their eyes closed. I didn't want to squeeze Mrs. Wingfield's hand too tight because it seemed like it would bust, but I also didn't want to appear wimpy. Their praying made me restless. The place smelled like an old person. There were lots of air fresheners. I checked out the faded wallpaper that was once probably pretty ritzy. I saw the chipped paint next to a light fixture on the ceiling and wondered how Mrs. Wingfield changed the lightbulbs.

When the prayer was over they each gave my hand a light squeeze and picked up their napkins and neatly placed them in their laps. It was creepy. Sarah flashed me a quick grimace.

After everyone had been served, no one uttered a word. All I could hear was the sound of myself chewing.

"This is real good food," I said.

"Yeah, Mom, thanks a lot," said Sarah.

Her mother nodded and after a long pause asked, "So how's everything in New York?"

"Everything's fine, Mom," Sarah said. She wasn't eating. I wondered if her mother knew Sarah was a vegetarian.

"Sarah has big dreams," Mrs. Wingfield calmly said to me. "Did she tell you that? She wants to be a singer."

"I've seen her sing," I said.

"She's good, isn't she?"

"Yes, she is," I said. I was trying to eat as much tuna as I could without seeming overzealous or making too big a mess.

"She wants to be 'special,' " she said, picking up her glass of Riunite.

"Mother," Sarah said with an artificially pleasant expression.

Her mother smiled back and continued talking.

"Did she tell you that I worked my whole life as a secretary in a real estate office, saving money for her to go to a good college?"

I shook my head no.

"I don't work there anymore. I'm retired." She took a big slug of her wine. "Did she tell you that I was valedictorian of my high school?"

I shook my head no.

"Mom, give it a break," Sarah said.

"Well, I was. But I didn't attend college. Sarah's father didn't deem it important that either one of us go to college. But she loves him. I guess she's told you all about him?"

"We actually haven't talked that much about things like that," I said, looking over at Sarah, hoping for some signal on how to proceed. She was just looking down in her lap, refolding her napkin.

"She's not much of a talker, is she?" Mrs. Wingfield said, looking over at her daughter, taking another healthy gulp of white wine. There was another long pause.

"Oh, Sarah, don't get in a mood. I'm not going to be bad. I'm just telling your young man a little information about us." She turned back to me. "Putting your daughter through college all by yourself is something to be proud of, don't you think?"

"Yeah, that's really great," I said, a little too cheerfully. I was trying to just keep eating.

"Where did you go to college, William?"

I paused, swallowed, and, careful not to seem embarrassed, said, "I didn't go to college, ma'am."

Mrs. Wingfield studied me, taking me in fully, holding her glass of Riunite as if it were a highball. I thought as long as I kept eating I couldn't get into too much trouble.

"Sarah's shy because she thinks she has bad legs," her mother announced. Sarah stopped moving entirely.

"But I used to pray every day for God to keep her legs a little chubby because women with nice legs give themselves permission to be uninteresting. I think that's true. Like me — I had attractive legs," she said, rubbing her knotty hand down one leg, which she crossed over the other leg, straightening out her dress. "But all it did was get me in trouble." She picked up her fork and began eating again. She looked over at me. "You're a little handsome for a husband," she continued. "A person has to be careful of handsome men. Because they drink."

"William is really enjoying your company, Mother. You're a real pleasure to be around," Sarah said quietly.

"My daughter doesn't like me," she said. "And sometimes I suppose I am unpleasant, but it's only because I don't get to see her nearly as much as I would like. I just miss her. She's a beautiful girl." Mrs. Wingfield stretched out her arm and began lightly fussing with Sarah's hair. "You can't trust love. Friendship, true friendship is all that you can trust. You'll see."

Sarah had both her hands hidden inside the sleeves of her blouse. She looked up at me and smiled an apology.

"You'll have to forgive my mother," she said. "She reads too much *Reader's Digest* and has a tendency to preach."

"Yes, but you see, I always believed in being 'of use,'" her mother said, standing up and pouring herself some more wine. "I would ask myself, How can I be of the most use? It is in that way that God speaks to us. And Sarah doesn't think about that. She wants to be special."

"I don't want to be special, Mom. A person can be 'of use' by singing. The world needs singers, doesn't it?" Sarah asked.

"Yes, but your mother doesn't," she said, pretending to be playful. "Your mother doesn't need any singers at all. And I think that New York has more than its share."

"Mom, you're drunk."

Mrs. Wingfield stared at her daughter. "Yes, I am. I have many faults, the worst of which is not how painfully I miss my daughter." She reached over again and straightened Sarah's collar. "But I will be able to stand before God and I'm a little worried about you."

"We'll see, Mom, we'll see," Sarah whispered.

"And what about you, Mr. William . . . What is your last name?" she asked, turning her gaze toward me. She had the cold, empty, gray eyes of a blind person. I realized that I hadn't spent much time with old people.

"Harding," I said.

"Well, Mr. Harding, will you be able to stand before God?" She smiled a big, drunk, pompous smile.

"Oh, Mother," Sarah instantly pleaded, putting her napkin up on the table.

I stared at her mother and I thought about what she asked me.

"To tell you the truth, Mrs. Wingfield, it's my opinion that I have stood before God since the moment I met your daughter."

After that we didn't talk at all anymore.

When supper was over, Sarah asked me to go wait outside on the front porch while they cleaned up.

The house was one of those ranch-style, single-floor homes, in a neighborhood with a couple hundred others exactly like it. It was dark out, but I could feel the presence of the thick, green trees that surrounded the house. No cars were on the street. The air was heavy and humid. Every now and again, I'd catch a glimpse of lightning bugs in the bushes. Hundreds of moths were swimming around the porch light like sperm. The house was blue, or at least it used to be. I waited out there for a while, not sure if it was all right to smoke a cigarette. I was pretty sure things were going terribly. I peeked my head back inside to see what was going on and I overheard Sarah and her mother talking over the rattle and clanking of dishes being washed.

"I just don't want you to get hurt," I heard Sarah's mother say.

"I won't," said Sarah.

They didn't speak for a moment.

"He looks like David."

"Oh, he does not."

"He smells like David," her mother said.

"He doesn't smell like him," hissed Sarah.

"He smells like something I don't like."

I was stunned. I sniffed my armpits. They smelled okay. I looked down at my khakis, and they were a lot more wrinkled than I'd noticed before.

I shut the door and stepped back outside.

When Sarah came out I was standing at the far end of the porch, away from the light and all the bugs. She stepped onto the wood floor carefully, shut the door, and peeked back through the window. Then she ran over to me, skipping like a schoolgirl, and tried to start making out with me, laughing and giving me big, slushy, wet kisses. I stopped her.

"You shut her up," she laughed. "I'm sorry about all the God business. She only does that when she drinks." Sarah wrapped her arms around my waist and stood up on top of my boots.

"This is not exactly the evening I anticipated," I said.

"I know, I know, I know, I know," she said. "But you're doing great." She smiled up at me, a big, hopeful grin to make sure I wasn't ticked off.

"I am?"

"Yes," Sarah said, squeezing one of my ears, teasing me. Then under her breath, in secrecy, she said, "Let's go make out."

"Wait a minute," I said, moving her off my feet. "Let me ask you a question."

"Okay, sure," she said, a shrinking expression washing across her face.

"Who's David?"

She froze.

"You heard that?" she murmured.

"Yeah."

"Nothing. Don't say his name, okay?" she asked.

"He's your old boyfriend?"

"Yes, but let's not talk about him now. Don't you want to mess around?" Sarah was lightly tugging at me to step off the porch.

"Listen, between finding out I smell like some guy named David and your mother in general . . . I ah . . . you know what I mean?"

"Oh, God." Sarah took a long, deep breath. She started grabbing at her wrists nervously. "Just don't think about those two, okay? Don't think about them at all."

"Someday, Sarah, you know you're gonna have to talk to me," I said. She was quiet.

"What did you mean by saying you saw God in me?" she asked.

"I don't know," I sighed, leaning over on the front porch railing. I looked out onto the mist of her front lawn. The air was thick; it made everything look grainy, like an old photograph. "Is it all right if I light a cigarette?"

"Sure," she nodded. She just wanted me to be having a good time. "Don't be mad, okay?" She tugged on my T-shirt.

"Here, sit down," she said, motioning that we both should seat ourselves on the edge of the porch and slip our legs in between the slats of the railing.

"David and I went out for three years in college," she began. I braced myself, trying not to reveal my instant loathing for this David person. "We lived together. After a while he said that he couldn't fall asleep with me in the bed with him. So I started sleeping in the living room on the couch. One night I heard a noise, so I walked into our bedroom and he had snuck another girl up the fire escape and was having sex with her in our bed." She paused. "The worst part about it was I didn't break up with him." She said all this facing out, her hands on her knees, and her legs gently swinging off the edge. "Moving all the way to Seattle was the only way I could really end it. You see, I'm not so tough," she said looking back at me. "I keep trying to tell you I'm what they call a dork."

It was quiet in Connecticut.

"Don't you find it odd," she continued, "that when you're a kid, everyone, all the world, encourages you to follow your dreams. But when you're older, somehow they act offended if you even try."

I wanted to tell her to follow any goddamn dream she could think of, but I knew I'd come off like a cornball.

"You should come to France with me," I said.

"What do you mean?"

I hadn't really thought about it before, but at that moment it seemed perfectly logical.

"Come to France," I said.

"I can't afford that, and neither can you," she said, giving me a real cockeyed look.

"They gave me a first-class ticket. I bet I could trade it in for two coach ones."

"I've never been on an airplane before," she said with pangs of terror in her voice.

"So come."

"I think I'm afraid to fly," she said.

"No, you're not."

"I can't go. You're going to have to work." She took my work more seriously than I did.

"Come on," I said.

"No," she said decisively, putting an end to the discussion. She stood up and quietly moved across the porch. "Come here, come here," she breathed in her most sultry voice. "Let's go fool around. I don't want to talk."

I flicked my cigarette out into the yard and ran toward her. My boots made big, heavy clunks across the porch.

"Shhhhh!" She moved back to me and took me by both my hands and led me quietly into the backyard. We hid under a colossal pine tree, where her fort had been when she was a kid. She lay down on a bed of pine needles and beckoned me to come to her. I knelt down over her and unbuttoned her blouse. Then, as slowly as possible, I pulled the straps of her bra down around her arms, unleashing her white shoulders. Her breasts were so pale they seemed to glow. She pressed her arms tight to her sides as she always did to prevent her breasts from falling. She wanted me to kiss her. I did. She was like a bird, safe and warm in her original nest. Pine needles lost in the tangles of her hair.

"Do you have a condom?" she asked.

"No," I said.

"Then we can't."

"Oh, God," I moaned.

"Shhh," she whispered. "You don't want me to get pregnant, do you?"

"Yes," I said.

"Don't say that."

"Okay, I won't." I kissed her neck. She looked up at our pine branch ceiling. I could feel her heartbeat through her skin; I thought I could hear it. For a moment, I felt myself calm in a way I'd never known. There was no nervousness in my entire body. I thought, if I could be inside her, I could die. I lay there awake, feeling her body for a long time, sure she was asleep.

"I wish I were old," she said, breaking the silence in a melancholy voice, "so I didn't have to worry so much about my future."

"When you're old," I said, "your future will be even more uncertain than it is now."

Walking back inside, creaking open the door, we found Sarah's mother still wide awake. She was seated cross-legged with one little light on, doing nothing but waiting for us. Mrs. Wingfield had made a bed for me by covering the couch with sheets.

She showed me to the bathroom where I was to get

"cleaned up." I hadn't brought a toothbrush or anything, so I just went in there and made a lot of noise. I could hear Sarah and her mother giggling in the other room. At one point Sarah snuck into the bathroom and quickly shut the door.

"I'll go to Paris with you if you still want, but we'll need to leave a week early and I'll come home before you have to start your work." She'd changed into a pair of old pajamas and was speaking formally.

"Okay?" she asked.

"Okay," I said.

"Well, then, good night." She walked over and kissed me on the cheek. Her lips were cool, wet, and clean. She gave me a warm smile and exited. As she turned around, I could see a few pine needles still lost in her hair.

N I N E

Here's how the story was told to me.

My mother and her best friend since the third grade, Danielle, were both sixteen and seated on the white plastic benches outside the Dairy Queen. Danielle had sleek black hair, whereas my mother's was dirty blond. Danielle was the beautiful one according to my mother. Danielle had breasts. They were watching the cars drive by Jacksboro Highway talking about what a "rat's hole" Fort Worth, Texas, was. After school, in Danielle's garage, the two girls had recently begun trying to teach each other how to rid themselves of their Texan accents.

It was fall of their junior year of high school. John Jaegerman pulled up in a Plymouth. John was Danielle's sometimes boyfriend.

"Hey, whatcha doin'?" John yelled from the passenger seat of the car. The girls didn't answer him. "Say, Jesse," he said to my mother, "how 'bout you talking Danielle outta bein' mad at me, and the both of y'all get in the car with me and Vince here — and we'll all take a spin into Dallas? Maybe drink some beers?"

"We got school tomorrow, stupid," my mother yelled over the sound of the engine, unable to avoid her accent.

It wasn't just Danielle who was sore at John Jaegerman.

John had black hair cropped in a high and tight crew cut. He always wore blue jeans with a blue jeans jacket. My mother and John were in the same biology class. The week before, they had had a test, and when the teacher left the room, John Jaegerman stood up, walked over to the teacher's desk, found the answer sheet, and proceeded to read aloud all the answers. John and my mother were the only two people who didn't get a one hundred on the test. My mother didn't because she was so disgusted with his behavior that she refused to listen. John didn't because when he sat back down he copied off my mother.

"Oh, come on, Jesse, we'll be back 'fore anyone gets in any real trouble," John said, getting out of the car and motioning for his friend to follow. His friend was tall and lanky, and it was difficult for him to maneuver his legs out of the driver's seat. He wore a white T-shirt over his skinny frame. His hair was shaggy. My mother thought he was the most attractive boy she'd ever seen.

"Y'all know Vince?" John Jaegerman asked. The girls didn't say anything. "Well, this here is Vince Harding." Then he turned to Vince and said, "Vince, this is Jesse, and that one there is Dan. But Dan is mad at me. Ain't that right, Dan?"

"I'm not mad at you, John Jaegerman. I'm just bored with you," Danielle said.

"Jesse, will you tell Dan that she's the only girl I'll ever love?" John said, grinning and sitting down next to my mother.

"Jesse," said Danielle, "will you tell John Jaegerman to please think of that the next time he decides to steal a car?"

A few weeks before, John had been caught with a stolen station wagon. Somehow he had talked the family he stole it from out of pressing charges.

"What about you, Mr. Vince? Do you talk?" my mother asked. Vince had just been standing there with his hands in his pockets, listening. Vince had graduated high school that spring and was biding his time waiting to start college down in Houston. My mother had seen him in school the year before but had never heard him speak. He usually hung out with the smart kids.

"I know a joke," he said, looking down, digging his boot heel into some dirt.

"Well, let's hear it," said Danielle. My mother didn't need to hear it. She was already dead bull's-eye in love. She listened to the sound of his voice, thinking what a good father he would make.

When the joke was over, no one laughed, but my mother said, "Come on, Dan, let's go to Dallas."

Vince kissed her good-bye that night on the front porch of her daddy's house, both their breaths stinking of beer. Eight months later I was conceived in the back of that very same Plymouth.

I was thinking a lot about that story. I wondered if sex was easier in Texas than in New York. I wondered how my father had talked to my mother. I wondered how other men in general behaved when they were alone with women.

Paris is where it all went down.

By the time we found a hotel, it was dark. The Hôtel de Nesle. Our room was at the top of six flights of a spiral stair-case, three flights away from the bathroom. It had a sink, a small table with a lamp, one chair, and a single bed. If we hadn't been so strung out, I think we would've liked it a lot. One wall was hand-painted with a cartoony image of a big, fat guy on a camel with lightning bolts coming toward him. Un-derneath the painting were the words "Saint-Paul sur le chemin de Damas." The opposite wall had a large window that opened out onto the street. Sarah sat Indian-style on the bed with her shoes still on, as if she were afraid of the floor.

This was to be the last week we spent together.

Sarah watched me tinker around the room and change my T-shirt. She wanted me to say something. A large fly of some kind was making a racket, flying and thumping into the over-head lightbulb. I took a swing at it with my shirt.

"Don't kill it," she said almost inaudibly.

We watched the thing buzz around. I realized that I had

never traveled alone with a woman before. I had the distinct feeling that we were playing some peculiar game of house.

"Do you ever feel other people's lives more palpably than your own?" she asked, still watching the fly.

"What do you mean?"

"Sometimes I can't feel my own life," she said in a despondent tone.

I didn't look over at her. I didn't want to have a huge conversation. "We're just tired," I said. I put my head in my hands, took off my glasses, and rubbed my eyes. "I'm gonna go wash my face." I made a move for the door.

"I think we should have sex tonight," she said.

"Oh, really?" I asked, turning around. "You decided this?"

"Yes, but I want to ask you some questions first."

"Ah . . . okay, shoot." I didn't know what was going on. I stood there and looked down at her, cross-legged on the bed. She was poking her hand inside her shoe, massaging her foot. She'd obviously been brooding over a plan.

"Do you have any diseases?" she asked, pulling in her shoulders and looking up at me, smiling a little.

"No," I said. "No diseases."

"Okay, good. Have you ever been baptized?" she asked.

"No," I said.

"You haven't?" she said, shocked.

"No," I said. "Do I fail the test?" I was really tired. I had spent the day lugging our bags across Paris. She didn't answer me.

"Why are you so scared to have sex?" I asked, standing above her.

She looked up at me. The fly was making the only noise in the room.

"I don't think God likes me very much," she said.

I couldn't figure out how to respond to that. I put my glasses back on. I didn't know what I'd been thinking, bringing her across an ocean. She looked frail. I could see how badly she wanted to be home.

"Look, why don't we just take showers and get some sleep, okay?" I started digging through my bag, trying to find some soap.

"Aren't you scared of dying?" she asked.

"Not really. I don't think so."

"I am," she said simply.

"If you believe in God, why are you scared to die?"

"I don't believe in God," she said. She was biting on a thick strand of her hair. "I'm not very much fun, am I?"

"Don't worry about it, all right? We'll have fun tomorrow." I was crouched over, rummaging through my things.

"William," she said. I turned and looked over. Her eyes were bright green. She stepped off the bed. She was wearing a black, floral dress that hung slightly past her knees, burgundy stockings, formal green leather shoes, and a small, tan button-up sweater. She reached up and took two silver barrettes out of her hair. She was holding herself stiff as if she were cold. "I want to have fun now," she said softly.

Slowly, she reached up and unbuttoned her sweater, pulled it off the length of her arms, and let it fall to the floor. She squeezed her shoulder and arm out from the neck of her dress, and then slid the dress over her other arm. The dress fell to her feet. I stood up. She was standing in the amber light of the room in only her black bra, silver necklace, burgundy tights, and her shoes. I put my hands in my pockets. I could see the white of her underwear through the sheer stockings.

Her stomach was folding awkwardly over the tight elastic around her waist. With her feet, Sarah gently pried off her shoes. She was watching me. She peeled her tights down to her knees, first taking out one leg, then the other. She promptly looked back up at me. I didn't say anything. She reached around her back and unfastened her bra, letting her white breasts fall open in the room. Her silver necklace lay in between her two large red nipples. She hooked her thumbs around her panties, bent over, and rolled them down to her ankles. She took two timid steps, unraveling her underwear off her feet, and then stood up. She was naked.

Her right foot was turned inward and her whole leg was almost imperceptibly shaking. I could see her chest moving in quick, fragile breaths. I wanted to hold her but I could feel my own heart beating fast. I brought my hands out of my pockets, walked toward her, and took hold of her wrists. I leaned down to kiss her. Her mouth was cold and rigid.

"Why are you doing this?" I asked her as gently as I could.

"Turn off the light," she said under her breath. "I want you to make love to me."

I turned off the light. She was still standing in the center of the room. I took off my pants and wrapped my arm around her back. I hoped that my hand felt strong to her. Sarah's skin was so clean to the touch. I could feel the smell of her hair all the way down in the bottom of my stomach. She was shivering as I laid her on the bed. Lifting up the sheets, she crawled underneath. I took off my underwear and eased myself in beside her. Her legs were cool. I tried to remind myself to breathe. Her necklace was tangled under her chin and looked as if it hurt her. I lifted the chain up through her hair and off her head. The room was black. I could feel Sarah holding her breath as I slipped inside her.

"Stop," she said, "stop. Get a condom. There's some in my purse."

I was surprised at how much forethought she'd given this night. I stood up to get the rubber, but I knew as soon as I did that I wasn't going to be able to have sex with her. I hate prophylactics. I was so nervous I couldn't even make a fist. I was thinking of a story Sarah had told me about the day her father moved away. When her older brothers told her their father was gone, she didn't believe them. She ran all through the house, searching in closets and under cupboards, thinking it was some kind of elaborate game of hide-and-seek.

I felt like there was so much blood in my head I had to lean over. My penis was in a fast retreat. When I got back into bed with the condom in my hand, I felt myself shrink up smaller than I'd ever thought possible.

"Fuck," I said out loud.

"What? What's wrong?" she asked, whispering.

"I can't do this," I said. I was forced into a complete reevaluation of myself. I was thinking about a guy my mother had dated who always called me a mama's boy. I hated him. I didn't want to be thinking about my mother. I could barely talk. My throat was all dry. I wanted to go into the bathroom and slam my head against the wall ten times.

"What is it?" she asked, sitting up in bed holding the sheets over her breasts. "Don't you want to have sex?" she asked, wiping her nose.

"Yes, I do. I just can't right now is all."

"Why not?"

I couldn't answer her. I wanted to disappear.

"Why not?" she asked again.

"Look, Sarah, let's just go to sleep." I rolled over and faced the wall. I could sense her still sitting up staring at me. After what seemed like an hour, I heard her say again, "What's wrong?"

I reached up and pulled her down next to me. For some reason I couldn't talk. I couldn't even think. I felt like the back of my skull would bust. I wondered why Sarah asked me if I'd been baptized. I wondered why I wasn't. I thought I'd call my mom about it when I got home. I looked up at the painting of Saint Paul on the wall. I wished I knew his story.

I lay awake for hours. Finally I could feel her breathing change and knew she was sleeping. Something about this girl was disassembling me. I stared at the ceiling and followed the cracks with my eyes.

One of her breasts was resting its weight on my chest. One of her legs had draped itself between mine. One of her hands was placed on my stomach. I kissed her on the cheek. Her whole body was warm now and smelled of sleep. I could feel myself relax. I kissed her neck. She was still asleep. I moved myself on top of her, pressing both her breasts against my chest. She leaned her head back into her shoulder. Her black hair made stormy patterns against the white pillow. I reached my hand around to the small of her back and placed my legs in between hers. She was still asleep. I kissed her mouth and eased myself inside her. She awoke. She took a wild, deep breath and kissed me. She reached both hands up around my shoulders.

"Are you wearing a condom?" she asked under her breath.

"No."

"It's all right," she said. "It's all right."

In the morning when I woke up, Sarah was watching me. She was sitting on the small wooden chair with her feet up on the bed. There was a towel covering her chest and a T-shirt twisted around her head. Her face was still wet and flushed from the shower. She looked like an Arabian princess. She had pushed the windows open. The room smelled sweet and clean.

"You're looking pretty sassy this morning," I said.

She bit her bottom lip, smirked, and looked away. I stood up naked on the bed and banged my chest Tarzan-style. She covered her ears.

"We're in Paris," she whispered as if it were a secret. I sat back down, put on my underwear, and looked out the window.

"Say it," I said.

"Say what?"

"You know, say it."

"What?"

"*How camest thou hither? The orchard walls are high and hard to climb,*" I told her.

"No," she said.

"SAY IT."

"Why?"

" 'Cause it'll be fun."

"All right: How camest thou hither. The orchard walls are high and hard to climb," she said, completely deadpan.

"*WITH LOVE'S LIGHT WINGS DID I O'ERPERCH THESE WALLS; FOR STONY LIMITS CANNOT HOLD*

LOVE OUT, AND WHAT LOVE CAN DO THAT DARES LOVE ATTEMPT; THEREFORE THY KINSMEN ARE NO LET TO ME." I belted this out to her with my arms outstretched from the window.

"Do you feel better now?" she asked.

The next few days were spent indoors, staying out of the rain. Steam would condense on the inside of the hotel window as raindrops dripped along the outside. The scent of sex was thick. I never wanted to take a shower again. My hands, my arms, my face all smelled of Sarah.

After sex once, I watched Sarah take the condom off me, tie it in a neat little knot, and throw it away. I was instantly overwrought with jealousy. Where did she learn how to do that? She went to take a shower and I was in misery. I wondered what she was thinking about and why she was taking so long. Why did she want to bathe? When she came back, all was forgiven.

She'd braid her hair and blithely talk about silly movies. We played thousands of hands of gin rummy. She'd sit in the window watching the rain and sing songs. I'd say sing "that one" again. We drank wine. She was an easy drunk. She would laugh unceasingly, her voice sounding smooth like the reed of a clarinet. We would mess around all day until it hurt. The air would get hot. We would sweat. It was hard to tell if she was kissing me or touching me; every part of her body was as wet as her mouth.

We weren't good tourists. When it stopped raining we hardly did anything except walk around. It was our first time in a foreign country. Even French Coke cans were thrilling. Sarah liked to walk on the curb while I walked on the street; that way we could hold hands and be the same height.

We saw an old woman screaming at her basset hound. The dog was just calmly drooling on the sidewalk and the woman kept bawling him out. Hey, lady, that dog doesn't speak French, I thought to myself. France was beautiful. Even the lights of the porno shops had class.

Sarah had brought along some money for the sole purpose of buying a dress. We found a used-clothing store, and I watched Sarah go to town. She'd grin at me each time she'd go back into the changing room. It reminded me of going shopping with my mom.

Whenever my mother would go clothes shopping, I would be miserable. Those were the times I missed my father. I'd wander around the mall by myself, pretending I was an orphan. That made me feel better. Orphans had no past. They could love people without being brought down by them. I'd steal a pack of Camel cigarettes and go outside and smoke them next to the older kids. I'd sprint through the center of the shopping area like I was Tony Dorsett of the Dallas Cowboys.

But with Sarah I was comfortable just hanging out. I would sit tranquilly and wait to comment on the forthcoming outfit. She decided on a black, sleeveless dress that came with long, black, elbow-length gloves. She also picked out an old, green suit for me and insisted that we go out that night for a big, snazzy dinner.

Ordering was fun. Sarah knew a little French — she had taken it for two years in high school — but I was helpless. We ordered cheese fondue. The walls of the restaurant were a deep shade of red, and our waiter had a perfect little wispy French mustache. The place was lit almost entirely by candlelight. It was precisely the French restaurant we might have

93

imagined. The waiter was nice but, I thought, a little over-friendly with Sarah. He kept touching her bare shoulder. She was sitting on the inside against the wall, and I was across from her.

"I think I was conceived the last time my parents had sex," Sarah said, dipping into her fondue, careful not to get any cheese on her gloves.

"My father went to a rehabilitation center in Albany one day and never came back. He was an alcoholic," she said. "But he wrote me once a week from the day he left, until I went away to college."

"What happened then?" I asked. In my suit, and with Sarah in her elegant dress, I felt like we were a true cosmopolitan adult couple.

"Once I was away at college he'd come visit me," she said. "He just didn't want to ever see my mother again. His letters were my favorite part of growing up. They always came in these dark blue envelopes and I'd keep them in a box underneath my bed. I loved that they were blue because when he lived with us, he'd come home always wearing his blue work shirt, and sit down in front of the television, and I'd sit on the back of the couch behind him and scratch his back. I'd scratch his back for as long as my mother would let me. When I'd go to bed at night my fingers would be stained blue."

"And you liked that?" I said.

"Yes, I did." She nodded her head and stroked her hair. Her hands were still wrapped in her long black gloves. She was happy there that night. I know she was. She looked at me and then around the dark room at all the other customers.

"Can you see me?" she asked.

"Yes," I said.

"Good," she said. Then surreptitiously she crossed her arms, with her hands resting at the top of her breasts, and slowly inched her sleeveless dress down underneath her breasts, still covering herself with her hands. I couldn't figure out what she was doing. Her eyes were bright and lascivious. She moved her hands away from her breasts, leaving them naked for me and all the world to see.

"Would you like me to scratch your back?" she said barely loud enough for me to hear.

"Yes," was all I could seem to say. I was suddenly insufferably uncomfortable in my new suit.

"You would?" she said. I nodded yes. All my blood was rushing to my face.

"Go to the bathroom," I said.

"Why?" she asked, giving me her most coy look, her breasts still open to plain sight.

"Just do it," I said. She inched her dress back up, straightened her gloves, and excused herself.

Sarah hid her face behind my back the entire walk home.

"Oh, my God," she kept saying. Then she'd look at me and hide her face again. Making love in the bathroom had been difficult. She was facing the sink and I was standing behind her. I still had my glasses on so I could see us in the mirror. Her face was red and blotchy. She had the breasts of a full-grown woman, and I could see my hand roaming across them. It didn't look like my hand. I felt like a puppy whose paws are too big for his legs.

We arrived back at the Hôtel de Nesle, and Sarah sat down on the bed with her formal outfit still on. She began unwrapping a chocolate mint that the housekeepers had left for us.

"Is it okay if I eat this?" she asked.

"Sure," I said.

"Don't you want it?" she asked.

"No."

"I shouldn't," she said. "I ate the one last night."

"Go ahead," I said, taking off my suit jacket.

"No, you eat it," she said, bringing it over to me.

"I really don't want it."

"I'm going to eat it," she warned.

"I want you to."

"You don't think I'll get fat?" she asked.

"No."

"Will you mind if I get a zit tomorrow?" she asked.

"How big will it be?"

"Not very," she said. Sarah was a girl who loved chocolate. She had eaten three chocolate crêpes earlier that day with this same debate preceding each purchase.

"Okay. I'll eat this one but then I won't have any tomorrow," she said. She sat back down and calculatingly ate the chocolate. She broke it into tiny pieces and put them into her mouth one by one.

Sarah wasn't sexy the way other people are sexy. Her body wasn't tight or taut or anything like that. She was funny the way watching people fall asleep on buses, with their heads continually dropping, then jerking back up, is funny. She was human, the most human person I've ever met, and that was sexy.

I had spent so much time as a kid pretending. My mother and I would go out to dinner and pretend we were a family. I'd sit there and wonder where my father was eating. With Sarah I didn't need either of them. We could start our own damn family.

"Let's get married," I said. I'd wanted to tell her that I loved her, that I loved everything about her. I loved the way she made me feel, even when that was miserable. I loved the way she bought a dress, the way she made love in bathrooms, the way she ate chocolate. I loved her mother, her drunk, blue letter–writing father. I loved every thought she ever had.

"If we got married, my mother would have a cardiac arrest," Sarah said, with chocolate smudged all over her teeth.

"All right, fuck it," I said. "Let's have a kid."

That was another thing. Every time Sarah and I had sex, I wanted her to get pregnant. I did. I thought it would be perfect: "Man finds self with pregnant woman."

"No babies," she said, taking off her gloves.

"All right, no babies," I said. "You want me to go get some more wine?" I knew if I stayed in the room too much longer I was going to tell her that I loved her. I wasn't sure that was such a hot idea. I was worried maybe she didn't feel the same way, and that'd be uncomfortable. I was having trouble standing still.

"I'd love some wine," she said, "but I don't want to go back outside."

"No, no, don't worry about it," I said. "I'll go get it."

"Are you sure?"

"Yeah." I still couldn't sit down.

"William, are you okay?" she asked, forcing me to look at her.

"Yeah, I'm good," I said. "I just need a breath of fresh air."

"Well, go and pick us up some wine, and maybe some orange juice for the morning."

"Yeah, good," I said, putting back on my jacket. "See you in a minute."

"Bye," she said. I walked out and closed the door. I was standing next to the spiral staircase. The hotel was quiet. I could hear the drone of the hall light, and a person fitting his key into a door several flights below. I decided to go back in and apologize for appearing weird.

When I opened the door, she was still sitting on the bed.

"What's going on?" she asked.

"Nothing," I said. "I'll be right back." I closed the door again, and walked back into the hall. Sometimes it was so hard to be around her. She opened the door after me and stepped out into the hallway in her bare feet.

"What are you waiting for?" she asked.

"I don't know. I just got this flash of nervousness all of a sudden." I was staring at her feet. Her toes were all scrunched up. The floor must have been cold, since it wasn't carpeted or anything.

"Kiss me," she said. I did.

"I love you," she whispered. I looked up from her feet.

"I love you, too," I said.

"Go get us some wine," she said.

"I'm on it," I said, bolting down the stairs.

"Don't forget the orange juice," she yelled after me.

I ran through the city. I wasn't looking for a place to buy wine. I just ran.

On our last morning in Paris we sat downstairs on the floor of the hotel lobby eating the complimentary breakfast. There was an absurdly large fat woman who owned the hotel seated at the front desk. Her name was Madame Simone. She was a teasing older lady who spoke much more English than she let on. Her husband was a skinny little guy who was running around serving everyone. Breakfast was from nine to nine-thirty, so most days Sarah and I missed it. There was a substantial circular table only two feet off the ground that all the guests were supposed to sit under. They had lots of ragged pillows and rugs provided for comfort. Several gray cats were skirting around. We were served coffee in bowls and given as much bread and jam as we wanted. It seemed pretty cheap to me, but it had its charm.

With us that morning was a thirty-year-old woman from Australia with a neck brace. Her name was Rose. Rose had been living in the Hôtel de Nesle all summer due to her accident back in June (she had tripped down the stairs at Versailles on her third day of what was supposed to be a summer-long jaunt across Europe) and was on quite friendly terms with Madame Simone. She was surprisingly cheery for a woman in a neck brace. Also present were two German sixteen-year-olds, a boy and a girl. Although I never heard them speak, I was convinced they were running away from home. Finally, there were three sorority sisters from Atlanta, Georgia, who had absolutely no concern for how loudly they spoke. I liked them though because they laughed constantly.

"I want to be a flight attendant. What do you want to be?" the prettiest one turned and asked Sarah.

"I really don't know," she said.

"Well, what do you do now? Are you in college?" the girl asked.

"I'm a nanny. I take care of someone's kids," said Sarah.

"Oh . . . neat," the girl said and went back to talking with her friends.

Sarah cleared her throat and then addressed the room.

"Does anyone know if it's possible for Americans to get married here in Paris, and, if so, how would someone go about doing it?" Sarah often gave the impression that her sentences were fully thought-out before she spoke.

I looked at her. I must have asked her to marry me twenty times in the last few days but I had no idea that she was seriously thinking about it.

The sorority girls fell silent. Rose looked up over her neck brace. The German couple didn't pay any attention. They just continued dipping their bread into their coffee.

"Are you two thinking of getting married?" Rose asked.

"Yes, we are," Sarah said. She still hadn't looked over at me.

"Oh, my gosh, that's wonderful," said one of the girls in a thick Georgia accent.

Sarah gave her a curt smile. Rose started speaking across the room to Madame Simone in French. Sarah and I watched them. Rose turned to Sarah.

"She says she thinks it's possible. When do you want to do it?" she asked.

"Today," Sarah said, stealing a glance over at me. I couldn't help but give a broad-faced grin.

"*Aujourd'hui,*" Rose yelled back at Madame Simone.

"*Aujourd'hui?*" Madame exclaimed and then started whipping off some more French in a feverish pitch. Sarah got a panicked look. After a brief discussion, Rose turned her whole body, protecting her neck, back to Sarah.

"She says if you go to the American embassy you can apply, and if that works out, there's a place a few doors down that she thinks will perform the service. But she's not sure all that can happen in one day."

"Thank you very much," Sarah said to Rose and Madame Simone. Madame Simone nodded and gave us a sideways look of disapproval. The Germans were still oblivious. The pretty sorority girl leaned over to Sarah.

"I have some makeup if you want?"

In the hallway, after breakfast, I trapped Sarah against the wall. She was wearing an oversized brown sweater.

"So whatcha thinkin' about?" I asked her.

"If you don't want to, it's no big deal. I just thought maybe we should actually do it," she said.

It was all I could do not to laugh.

"I didn't say I didn't want to do it. I said, 'Whatcha thinkin' about?'"

"Look, I don't know," she said. She was speaking fast, making quick half-drawn gestures, looking up at me and then back down at the ground. "I'm just not sure if I can be away from you. And you joke about it, but how often in a person's life do they actually want to marry somebody? And I do — I'd like to marry you. I figure as long as we maintain a sense of ourselves as individuals and don't just become some sloppy, drivelly couple whose lives revolve around each other, then, you know, maybe it'd be better if we did get married. Because that way, if anything gets weird or something goes wrong, which, you know, it most likely will, we'd have to work it out. One of us couldn't just run away."

"Do you want to have a kid?" I asked.

"Not right away. No, I couldn't do that," she said.

"No, of course not right away," I said. I figured I'd work on her later. We looked at each other for a couple seconds. Some people walked into the hotel and made their way to the front desk.

"So, what do you think? Am I delirious?" she asked, straightening her sweater.

"Let's do it," I said. I was confident in my decision.

"What?" she asked. Her green eyes were huge. She looked at me, like I imagined she had looked at the first boy who ever asked her to dance.

"I want to do it," I said.

"Are you sure? You have to be sure. I mean, if we do this, we'll be mentioned in each other's obituaries, no matter what."

"Let's get married, let's be individuals, fuck it, let's break all the rules." I was getting a little carried away. I kissed her and moved my hands underneath her sweater.

"I have to call my mother," she said. "Do you want to call yours?"

"No. My mother respects spontaneity more than courtesy."

We walked to the hotel pay phone. I figured out the country access codes, and Sarah called her mother collect. I stood there next to the phone and looked around. One of the old, gray cats was swatting at a roach on the floor. The roach was trying to escape, but the cat was only toying with it, prolonging death. I couldn't believe this was the day I was getting married. It was perfect. This was our story.

"Hi, Mom, it's me," Sarah said, quickly pulling on my shirt. "No, Mom, I'm not dead." Sarah gave me an exasperated look. "I'm having a great time. I simply forgot to call, that's all." We both waited as her mother spoke for a while. "No, we didn't go there. . . . I don't know — we went other places. . . . Listen, Mom, I called for a reason. William and I are going to get married." Sarah bit her lower lip and gave me an anxious stare. "Mom? . . . Mom? . . . Hello? I know it's fast but it's what we want. . . . No, Mom, talk to me for a minute. . . . Yes, he's right here, but talk to me for a second." She put her hand over the receiver and asked me, "Do you mind talking to her?"

I shook my head no and took the phone. "Hello, Mrs. Wingfield?" I said. I wasn't nervous at all.

"So you want to marry my daughter," she said. It was a surprisingly good connection. I could hear her clearly.

"Yes, ma'am, that's right, I do." I was looking at Sarah. She had both her hands gripped tightly to the front of my flannel shirt.

"First of all," Mrs. Wingfield said, "stop calling me ma'am. You sound insincere."

"All right, that's a deal," I said. I liked this old lady. She had my number.

"She's not pregnant, is she?" she asked.

"No. Sarah doesn't want any babies."

"Well, good. I didn't have Sarah until I was forty-six. So that myth about young mothers having pretty babies isn't true, you understand?"

"Yup, I understand." Sarah was leaning her ear close to the phone, trying to listen.

"Now, listen, William. I want to be clear that I think you are both very stupid. Am I clear about that?"

"Yes, I think you are," I said.

Sarah moved in front of me and very quietly asked me what her mother was saying.

"It doesn't look like there's anything I can do about it, William," Mrs. Wingfield went on. "So feel free — marry my daughter."

"Thanks," I said.

"Now give me back to Sarah."

"Bye, Mrs. Wingfield."

"Bye, William," she said. I gave the phone back to Sarah. I was exhilarated.

Sarah took the phone and held it with both hands.

"Hi, Mom," she said. Sarah stood there listening to her mother for what seemed like far too long a time. She was getting an unsettled look on her face. She kept nodding and then tucking her hair behind her ears.

"Okay, Mom, we have to go," she finally said. "Yes, I understand . . . okay, bye . . . okay, bye . . . okay, bye." Sarah hung up the phone and stared at it.

"What'd she say?" I asked.

"I can't get married," Sarah said, still looking at the phone.

"What'd she say?" I asked again. Sarah turned around, put a knuckle into her mouth and spoke methodically through her hand.

"She said . . . she thought it was a good idea. She said that you'd be good for me. She was surprised, because she didn't think that you would like me for very long." Sarah smiled and shook her head.

We stood in silence.

"I'm sorry, William," she said. "I was being ridiculous." I looked around at the hotel. I was baffled. We had to move out of the way of some new guests that were carting their luggage up the staircase. I couldn't think of anything to say at all. Sarah was staring at me with absolutely no expression.

"Come here," I said. I took her hand and tried to lead her out of the hotel.

"No," she said. "I don't feel like going anywhere."

"Come on," I said.

"William, I can't get married."

"I know," I said. "Just for two seconds. Follow me."

I led her out onto the street. The ground was still littered with garbage from the night before. We could see the cleaning crews dressed in their neon-green outfits walking around picking up trash. Paris is much cleaner than New York. I walked fast, holding Sarah's hand.

"Where are we going?" she asked.

"You'll see," I said. We walked over Pont-Neuf and through the low-hanging gray clouds. The wind was blowing like a hurricane. Sarah was hanging on to me with one hand and using the other to pull her sweater up tight around her throat. Her hair was twisting around her face and into her mouth. We walked to Île de la Cité and onto the cobblestone courtyard in front of Notre-Dame. The tourists were already assembling en masse. There were screeching leaders escorting large groups off buses. There were families with boys and girls in Batman T-shirts. There were lots of people selling things.

I walked up to the entrance of the church and swung open the heavy door. In the front passageway Sarah stopped and let go of my hand. I turned to her. She reached out and fit her hand along my neck, straightened my hair, and lightly kissed me.

We walked into the cathedral. There were a few men and women seated on the pews deep in thought. I wondered what their prayers were. Some others were placing their five-franc pieces in the little metal box and lighting candles. Mostly there were people ambling about with cameras strapped around their necks. I could hear Sarah's and my footfalls echoing from above us. We walked down the aisle through the center of the church. The whole cathedral was lit in a warm, bluish wash. Giant stained-glass windows stood strong in every wall. I couldn't help but wonder about who set every stone and placed each pane of glass. We could hear a mother at the opposite end of the building trying to quiet down her children. Sarah reached over and grabbed my arm.

Close to the altar there was a heavy, red-velvet rope blocking our path. I lifted it up, and Sarah and I crawled under it into the restricted area. I knelt down at the altar. Sarah took one last look at our setting and knelt beside me. She gave me a soft peck on the cheek. There was a baroque golden crucifix hanging in front of us.

"What should we say?" I whispered. Sarah shrugged her shoulders. After a moment of silence, I heard her speak.

"Do you take me, to have and to hold, to love and to cherish, to the end of your days?"

"I do," I said. "And do you, Miss Sarah Wingfield, take me to love . . ." For some reason my mind was drawing a blank. I couldn't think of any other piece of the vow.

"I do," Sarah said. "Me, too."

Still on our knees, I took her face in both my hands and kissed her. A deep, wanton kiss. She lifted up her hands and left them hanging close-fisted in the air.

"Promise me," she said, "if anything goes wrong, if I ever run away or anything, you'll find me and force me to come back and kiss you."

"Nothing'll go wrong."

"You'll be gone four weeks. That's a long time," she said.

"I promise."

ELEVEN

I spent more than half the money I made in Paris on telephone calls to New York and on a Concorde plane ticket home. I took the Concorde so I could get home five hours earlier. No shit. I really did that.

It'd been four weeks since we had seen each other. I ran over to her house. I had flowers and a neatly wrapped box in one hand. In the other I held a towel I'd stolen from the hotel. It was getting cold. I could almost see my breath. Every couple of blocks, I'd slow down and try to make myself walk, but soon my walk would turn into a jog and I'd find myself sprinting again.

Her building looked different. All kinds of construction was going on outside it. Big guys with big belts and coffee cups were staring at me. I was panting in front of them, with flowers, a gift-wrapped present, and a towel. I tried to catch my breath and ignore them.

Sarah wasn't expecting me until the evening. I played through the several possible scenarios of our reunion. I'd ring her bell, she'd buzz me in, I'd run up the steps, she'd race down, the two of us would meet on the landing between the second and third floor and fall down in a fit of mad ecclesiastical passion. I imagined an alternate version. She'd leave her door open and I'd slowly peek my head in — only to find her standing on top of the bed buck naked. I'd throw her presents to the floor, pick her up, and swing her around in circles, until we fell to the floor in a fit of mad ecclesiastical passion. Mad ecclesiastical passion was the key.

Then I got scared that she might not actually be home. I rang the buzzer. A moment passed, then another. I rang the bell again. It was eight o'clock in the morning. I was sure she'd be home.

"Hello?" I heard her sleepy voice say through the intercom. I froze. I stared at the little mechanical device.

"It's the plumber. I've come to fix the sink," I said.

The intercom was quiet. I stood there breathing. I wondered if she could identify my voice. I looked over at the construction workers. I looked at the door. The buzzer sounded. She'd recognized me. I walked in. I went up the steps slowly. I wanted to give her time to run down and kiss me or get naked or whatever. I looked up the stairs, hoping to see her peering down, but I didn't see anything. I only heard the sound of my own feet shuffling. I wondered if that noise was familiar to her. At the top of the steps, I looked over and saw that the door had been opened an inch. I was out of breath again. The hallway was lifeless. No hidden shape could be seen moving through the crack. I thought for a second that I could hear music but then it was gone. I knocked gently but heard nothing. I pushed open the door and called out her name.

"Sarah?" I said, my voice dropping in the air.

"Yes," she said in a timid voice. I couldn't see her. There was a narrow passageway at the entrance to her apartment. I had to walk past the bathroom and around a corner before the whole kitchen-dining-bedroom came into view. I poked the flowers around the corner first. Then slowly, I peeked my head out. And there she was, standing against the opposite wall, next to a bowl of steaming oatmeal, staring at me. She didn't move.

"How ya doin'?" I said, with the flowers, present, and towel still in hand.

She was dressed in pajama bottoms and her gray cotton T-shirt with the picture of the Soviet flag. Her hair looked like it always did when she woke up, half of it matted down and the rest flying loose.

"I came home early," I said. She didn't say anything.

We were still standing on complete opposite sides of the room. She was looking at me as if I were an assassin.

"I wanted to surprise you," I said. "I thought it'd be fun."

"I'm eating oatmeal," she said. It was her first full sentence.

"Yeah, I can see. How is it?" I asked.

There was a long pause. Sarah looked at me, then at the oatmeal, then back at me.

"Pretty good," she said.

I held up the flowers.

"I got you these," I said. I shuffled over to her slowly and presented them. She took them, careful not to touch my hand.

"Thank you," she said, taking a step away from me. She inhaled the flowers' scent but never stopped examining me. It was as if there were a glass wall between us.

"I brought you the towel that you wanted," I said.

"Oh, thanks." She tried to smile.

"And here's a present," I said, handing her the wrapped box. "It's a green dress," I said before she had a chance to even look at it. "I saw it on a mannequin and it reminded me of the one you always wear, so I bought it. I don't know if that's lame or not, buying something for somebody that you know they already have, but it made sense at the time."

"Thank you," she said. She didn't open it.

"No problem."

We were silent again. I was starting to feel light-headed. I didn't understand why we weren't kissing. She was studying me like she didn't know who I was.

"Do you want to put those flowers in some water?" I asked.

"Yeah, sure," she said, motionless. She was holding the flowers tightly with both hands.

"Are you nervous?" I asked.

"Uh-huh," she mumbled.

"About seeing me?"

"Your hair is longer," she said. Her oatmeal was still steaming on the small table beside her. "You said you weren't arriving till tonight?"

"I wanted to surprise you."

"Oh, well, you did." She tucked her hair behind her ears. I wanted to try and kiss her but I thought if I did, she might catapult out the window.

"I took the Concorde," I said with pride.

"Isn't that expensive?" she asked. She was seeing the wrong side of everything. She was poised to run. I didn't know what to say.

"I heard a joke on the plane," I said desperately. "You wanna hear it?"

She made no sign. I went ahead anyway.

"Okay. There's these two monks, okay? A monsignor guy and a regular monk guy, and they're fishing." I was getting wound up, standing in the middle of her apartment performing for her.

"And the regular monk catches this humongous fish. He goes, 'Wow, that is one heck of a sonofabitch,' and the monsignor guy says, 'My son, watch your language,' and the other one says, 'No, Father, I'm sorry, but that's the name of the fish, "sonofabitch." 'Oh,' goes the monsignor."

I could tell already that she wasn't going to laugh.

"So that night they were initiating some new monk and they decided to serve the fish." I didn't know why I'd chosen such a long joke.

"They all sat down eating this fish and the regular monk guy goes, 'Boy, this sonofabitch is really good,' and the monsignor says, 'Yeah, I've never had sonofabitch this good,' and he turns to the new recruit and says, 'How do you like the fish?,' and the new guy says, 'Hey, I'm not much for fish, but I sure am going to enjoy working with you fuckin' guys.' "

She stared at me. I shrugged my shoulders in apology.

"I need to go to the bathroom," she said, and made a move to step around me. I reached for her. Her hand was hot and clean. She stopped and faced me.

"How ya' doin'?" I asked.

"I just woke up," she said.

I kissed her. With my smelly jeans, my jet-lagged eyes, and an overanxious mind, I placed my lips on hers. At first she was wooden, but before long she relaxed her shoulders and returned the kiss. She tasted of warm brown sugar and oatmeal. I held my hand strong against her braless back. When we stopped kissing, she eased her head onto my shoulder. I wasn't sure if the situation had corrected itself.

"Hold on a second," she said. "I still have to go to the bathroom."

I took the flowers and put the ends in the kitchen sink. Sarah bustled off to the bathroom. I ran the water, looked for a vase of some kind, and tried to tell myself that everything was going fine. I wished I could start over and take the right flight, take a shower, buy a nicer gift — something that cost a little bit of money maybe.

Then a thought occurred to me. She was probably getting undressed in the bathroom and would most likely come out stark naked. It was clear to me that there was nothing she could do that would make me not be in love with her and that she probably felt the same way about me. I pictured her walking out of the bathroom naked, her hands over her breasts, her cold feet slapping against the hardwood floor. I had spent the last few weeks yearning to see her naked. I'd even pleaded with her to send me nude Polaroids, but she'd only laughed. I tried to make myself loosen up. I took off my glasses and cleaned them with my shirt. I didn't want to be all freaked out and tense and not be able to have sex.

I wondered what it'd be like to make love to her again. I imagined her wet eyes, her belly, her hard, red nipples. I was glad it was getting cold out. I didn't want to go outside.

I never saw her naked again.

TWELVE

Sarah sent me five letters while I was away. This was the last.

W —

On the 7,691st day of my life, I can think of only a handful
I can remember. One of them was on a bus. I was on my
way to the first grade in a stiff, burgundy, floral dress and
pigtails. The bully girl, Gillian Boyd, was sitting next to me
eating my lunch. I wasn't doing anything except saying,
"Yes, have as much as you want."

A shadow fell across both of us. Sean McQuarrie. I don't
remember what happened, but he must have grabbed
Gillian by the collar and hurled her to the back of the bus.
She only glared at me after that. For the rest of the year I
rode all the way to school next to Sean, blushing and in love
at age six. We never forget our heroes.

It's Tuesday now. Thank you for singing into my answering
machine last night. I think you should come home soon.

When I pass mail people on the street, I stare at them and wonder if they have seen you. I am sleeping in my clothes again.

I look at all my trinkets from France — the matchbooks, the plane tickets, the hotel key — and I imagine my children finding them in an attic one day. They'll rush downstairs to ask me what they are — and I'll snatch them from their grubby little paws and reprimand them for being so nosy. I'll think then exactly as I do now — where have you gone? Have you met many exciting people?

love,

S

She'd sent three letters the first week and two the second. The third and fourth weeks she stopped writing entirely. We still talked on the phone almost every day. I'd tell her how tedious making a movie was and she wouldn't believe me. I saw any success I had as an actor as the mark of my greatest character flaw. The one thing I was good at was pretending to be someone else. I was disappointed that there was a market for it.

Sarah would talk about how much she hated missing me and that she loathed feeling needy. I was happy to have someone to miss.

When I was younger, adults were always telling me that I missed my father, but I thought they were all turkeys. My father had promised me that when I was thirteen I could come and live with him. I patiently waited out that date. On my thirteenth birthday he called, but he neglected to make any mention of our plans. I decided he could go fuck himself.

The next day, I got into a fistfight with Tommy Vitello. He broke my nose and I cracked his jaw. With the fight and with what the guidance counselors dubbed "atrocious grades," my mother sent me to a child psychologist. He asked me if my broken nose had anything to do with my conversation with my father. I told him the only reason I had a broken nose was because Tommy Vitello was an asshole. He told me two things: that I needed positive male role models and that I had a language problem. He was right.

In New York, my first night back, Sarah and I were lying in bed together. She didn't want to fool around. She said she had a stomachache. She told me how funny it was that she felt like she didn't know me anymore. Very funny, I thought.

The next evening, when I knew she'd be home from work, I went back over to Sarah's. She had a typewriter pulled out into the center of the floor and plugged into the wall. She was sitting over it writing something. She was a good typist. I figured that was something that probably everybody at college learned.

"Whatcha writing?" I asked her.

"Nothing," she said. She didn't stop to get up and say hi or kiss me or anything. She was just diligently working. The typewriter was making a loud hum along with the rattling of the keys. I sat down and waited for a while. I tried to make small talk, but she only gave me short answers. Her apartment was cold. The windows were wide open even though it was only about forty-five degrees outside. She was in an oversized collegiate sweatshirt, so I suppose she was warm.

"Well, I guess you're busy. I'll get out of your hair," I said, standing up.

"Okay, sure," she said, completely immersed in her typing. "I'm sorry. Why don't you call me later?"

"Yeah," I said. "I'll call you later." I ambled my way out of her apartment. When I closed the door behind me, I heard the tapping of her typewriter stop. She'd been waiting for me to leave.

On my third day home, I was sitting on Sarah's couch watching her pack. She was traveling up to Boston with her band to sing at some club and I was planning on going with her. She was flitting around her apartment, from the bathroom to the closet back to her overnight bag. She had asked me several times if I was sure I wanted to go with her.

"Maybe it'd be better if I didn't come," I said.

"Why not?" she asked.

"Well, it seems like you need some space. And you're right; I've got some things I should probably take care of." That was a full-blown fabrication. Now that the movie was over, I scarcely had a life at all. Outside of obsessing about Sarah, all I did was sit in bookstores and go to the movies.

"Okay, yeah, good. I think you're right," she said, folding a T-shirt.

"What do you mean?" I asked.

"I don't know. You just said you have some things to do."

"Yeah, but you know that's a fuckin' lie," I said. I knew I shouldn't have used the word "fuck"; it made me sound angry. "I mean, what is it? You don't want me to come?"

"I don't know. It's just . . . you don't seem to do anything except wait around for me. And that's not the kind of couple we wanted to be. I mean, you should take care of yourself and I'll take care of myself. It seems like we're turning into an ordinary couple, and you know that's not what I want."

"I do?" I said. This information was coming at me far too fast.

"Since you've been gone — I mean, I don't mean to belittle the time we spent in France, but it wasn't very realistic, you know? I need time for me, and sometimes you take that away." She was being deliberate with her packing and casual with her speech.

"I take that away?"

"I mean that I don't want to be just someone's girlfriend. I can't let my life revolve around you. I came here to be on my own. I'm just happy that I was able to feel the way you made me feel. I didn't think that was possible." She half laughed as she said that. I half smiled back.

She was feeling good, happy to have all this off her chest. She zipped up her overnight bag and looked at me. I was sitting there on her couch. It was the kind of sofa that looked like its previous owner had had a dog. My butt sank deep into the cushions, and I felt about three years old. I nodded like I was understanding and said, "So what's going on here? Are you breaking up with me?"

"I think we need some space," she said.

"Some space? You can think of something a little more original than that, can't you?" I asked.

"I'm just trying to tell you the truth." She had an indignant look on her face.

"Well then, you're a pretty boring person if catchphrases from Breakup 101 are your idea of truth." I tried to laugh at my own joke.

"Listen, I like you a lot —"

"Oh, great, you like me? So I don't have to feel bad then. Super. You think I'm a nice guy, a fun fella to hang out with in France, but not somebody to see on a day-to-day basis."

She'd clammed up and was sitting on the mattress, next to her bag, with her eyes to the ground. "What are you thinking?" I asked.

"You can't talk to me like this," she said.

"Oh, fuck you," I said. "You're the most selfish, spoiled, cold, bullshit coward. I've done what you're doing before — I've told people to fuck off, and I know how important you feel. I've been you, and I know that you suck."

THIRTEEN

The morning after Sarah returned from Boston, I was dressed in a tuxedo, standing five flights below her window, singing a different tune, and it went something like "I'm sorry."

It was eight o'clock in the morning when I woke up. I knew Sarah had to be at work by nine, so I put in my contacts, got dressed in my thrift-store tuxedo, and headed over to her window. I could see the flowers I'd given her sitting on her windowsill. I walked over, and, careful not to dirty my dresswear, picked up an orange construction cone that was sitting on the street. I put it to my lips and began to howl like a wolf. She knew who it was and came to the window with an inscrutable expression. I thought that she must be impressed. Girls loved shit like this.

She motioned to me that she'd be right down. I tried to give her a smile that she could see from five flights away, and then let out one final mammoth howl.

When Sarah walked out she was wearing a bright-red rain jacket with a hood. I could tell she was pissed.

"Oh, come on," I said to her scowling expression. Still holding the fluorescent orange cone, I pointed to my tuxedo. "How do you like my outfit. . . . It's my 'I'm sorry' outfit."

"It's nice. Why are you wearing it?" she asked, immediately beginning to walk down the sidewalk.

"Because I'm sorry."

"Look, I have to go to work," she said.

"I know. Can I walk you?"

It was a cool November morning and we both had hair that was still damp from the shower. She didn't have any stockings on and her legs were all pink and prickly. So was her face. The cold light made her eyes look fiercely green. I wondered again if she was Irish. I couldn't believe I didn't know.

"Are you Irish?" I asked.

"What?" she asked. She was walking with purpose.

"Nothing," I said. "Okay, so here's the deal. I'll do the talking, all right? Because I have some things to say and because you don't look particularly talkative. Not that you don't look good, because you do. That's why I asked the thing about if you were Irish.

"Anyway, I'll start the talking but if you feel like jumping in, you just say 'Hey, I want to talk,' and I'll probably say 'Go right ahead.' "

Needless to say she was mute. She was only walking.

"Okay. I know what you're thinking: God, this guy is a creep. Two days ago he tells me all kinds of nasty things, leaves my apartment in a huff, and now he wakes me up in the morning in an ugly three-cent tuxedo, howling at my window, and expects me to think it's funny. Well, let me tell you something, missy, you're absolutely right. I don't even like myself."

This was "A" material. I felt good. I was on a roll. We kept walking.

"So, what — the tux gets no comment? 'Where did you get that?' or 'Oh, you're so zany,' or maybe 'I can't believe you're such a cuckoo-head.' Nothing. You're just going to keep walking. Okay, that's cool.

"You want to know why I wore it? An attempt to make movies more realistic. I like to embrace the cliché." She wasn't responding. "I'm sorry, I'm sorry, I'm sorry. Nobody likes me, so don't feel bad. You're in the majority." Her walk was slowing slightly as I rattled away. I started to walk backward so that she'd be forced to look at me.

"You switched gears on me; you have to admit that. How am I supposed to respond? You're getting a little scared that maybe we went too fast and that's okay. It's just that you have to give me a little time to get used to the idea."

She grabbed my arm before I bumped into someone. "Thank you," I said. "I don't know how to love you right. You've got to let me know." I took a deep breath. "See, this is the way I see it, if the attempt is all, then I can promise you everything."

I stopped walking, praying that she would stop as well.

"I DON'T WANT A BOYFRIEND," she cried, and evaporated into the merging crowds of Third Avenue.

I froze. I'd never heard her raise her voice before. It was as if she had reached her arm inside my mouth, grabbed the bottom of my stomach, and ripped it out through the back of my throat. I wanted to snatch her hair and swing her around on the goddamn street. I could see my reflection in a glass building. I stopped and looked at myself. People were shuffling, swirling around me. I was five days shy of my twenty-first birthday. I wondered where everyone was going.

FOURTEEN

I went to twelve movies in the next three days. It was the only way not to watch the answering machine.

On the third day, I found myself at a pay phone outside her building. It was a little after midnight. She usually went to bed early on Sundays, but I'd convinced myself she might want to go get a cup of coffee. I imagined us sitting in a diner, nursing our coffee, and slowly beginning to smile about the last week's events. "Can you believe I said that?" I'd laugh. "Well, I thought you were mad at me," she'd say, blushing with relief. "But I thought you were mad at me!"

"Hi, it's me. I was wondering . . ." My voice was shaking. "Sorry for calling so late, but I thought if you wanted, we could go get a cup of coffee?"

"Uh, yeah . . . no, I think I'm too tired," she said.

"Well, sure, it's late."

"Yeah, I should go to bed," she said.

I couldn't let her go.

"How ya been?" I asked.

"Fine."

"Whatcha been doin'?"

A fire truck drove by with its sirens screaming.

"Where are you?" she asked.

I was startled. I didn't want her to know I was right outside her door, but she must have heard the fire engine from outside her window and over the phone.

"I'm uptown," I said, cringing at my own lie.

"Oh" was all she said. There was a long, awful pause.

"Are you singing anytime soon?" I asked.

"No . . . listen, uh, I should go to bed."

"Yeah, of course. . . . I'll talk to you later."

"Sleep well," she said.

"Okay, yeah, you, too."

"Good-bye, William."

"Bye."

I held on to the phone like it was a piece of her. Everything was disintegrating so quickly. I walked over and stared up at her light. I wished it would rain. I knew I was a dopey guy standing out in the cold staring up at a warm window, but it's so hard to miss someone who only lives eight blocks away.

FIFTEEN

The day before my birthday Sarah called and said she wanted to see me. I was elated. She told me she had birthday presents for me, but that she'd be too busy to see me on my actual birthday. She wondered if I could come by that night. I said, "Yeah, sure, that'd be great."

Her rehearsal was finished at ten and she suggested that I come by at eleven. At ten-thirty I sat down in a pizza place around the corner from her and waited. I wanted to be prompt.

She looked exquisite. She wore a solid-brown dress with white lace around the cuffs and the collar, her silver heart hanging from her neck, and one of those little red-plastic combs in her hair.

"I'm not quite ready yet," she said, letting me in. She was cordial but wasn't looking me in the eye.

"Do you want a beer?" she asked.

"Sure," I said.

"I think there's one in the fridge. Why don't you get it out?" She scrambled back toward the bathroom, hiding something behind her back. "I have to finish wrapping," she smiled.

ETHAN HAWKE

I opened the refrigerator, looked at all her rabbit-type food, and took out the one lone Rolling Rock Light. I used to feel so comfortable in her apartment. Now, I couldn't shake the feeling I was looking at everything for the last time. She had spices (rosemary, cinnamon, sage, etc.) all lined up on her sink. I wondered when she got those. I'd never seen a guy's apartment with spices.

"You can put on some music if you'd like," she called out from the bathroom.

"Okay," I said. I looked over at her tapes for a second. I didn't know what she wanted to hear and I certainly didn't want to be responsible for setting the mood. I sat down on her slumped-out couch. My ass sank well below my knees. I was mentally preparing myself for anything that might happen. I'd be tough.

She came out of the bathroom. She was in good spirits.

"How was your day?" she asked.

I wanted to leap up and say, "So what's the deal? What's going on? Why don't you want to see me?"

"Oh, fine," I said meekly, still lost inside Sarah's couch. "How was your day?"

"Crazy." She rolled her eyes. I couldn't believe how casual she was acting. "I've been ridiculously busy lately," she said.

Resting three bizarrely wrapped presents on the coffee table between us, she sat down on the floor and crossed her legs.

"So what are these?" I asked.

"Presents." She looked at me. It was our first eye contact since I'd come in.

"I guess I should open them, huh?" I asked.

She nodded with enthusiasm. It was strange — I remem-

ber that she was actually excited about giving me these presents. I couldn't fathom why. I opened the first two presents
in silence. They were two wine bottles dripped with wax.

"They're for candles," she said.

"Oh, how nice," I said, still waiting for the punch line to
this joke.

"And here are the candles." She stood up and got them
from a drawer in the kitchen.

"Thanks," I said.

She sat back down and handed me the big present. Her
face was full of anticipation. This could have been a beautiful
moment, if I hadn't been wrestling with the desire to smash
the table and cry out, "WHAT IS GOING ON?"

I opened the next present. It was a painting, a framed
painting that she had made. It was a sloppy portrait of a
bleeding heart, done in eight thousand shades of green, with
one spill of red that dripped down onto the frame. I loved it.
I held it in my arms. I stared straight down at it.

"Why did you give this to me?" I asked.

"I thought you'd like it," she said with genuine tenderness.

"I do." I took a pause. I couldn't swallow. I made myself
take a breath. "Do you want to keep seeing me?"

"I just don't think that now —"

"Then why did you give it to me?"

"What do you mean?" she asked.

"What am I supposed to do with it? Hang it on my wall?" I
couldn't look at her.

"I don't know, I thought —"

"You think I want to hang a picture on my wall, to remind
me of a girl who doesn't want to see me anymore?" All my
blood was now in my head.

"I warned you that I didn't think I could do this," she said, taking on the tone of a dental assistant.

"You also made me promise to force you to stay with me." I looked at her. "How am I supposed to do that?"

"You can't," she said, shaking her head. "I came here to New York to be on my own."

"Yeah, I know the story." I was clenching my fists, digging my nails into the palms of my hands.

"I'm just trying to be honest."

"Well, I wish you'd lie a little bit."

"You want me to lie?" she asked. She gave me this quizzical look as if I were the one behaving irrationally. That pissed me off.

"No, I just want you to appear. We're apart for four stupid weeks —" I stood up "— and I come back to this? What did I do?"

"Look, if you really do care about me, then you should see —" She was attempting to calm me down.

"This is my fault?" I asked.

"It's no one's fault."

"Well, that's debatable," I said, standing above her.

"I told you that this would be difficult for —"

"Would you shut up with the lines? You don't like me anymore. You don't want to go out. It was fun for a while. Now it's not fun so I should go away and HANG YOUR FUCKING PICTURE ON MY WALL."

She looked down and covered her eyes with her hand. She was still seated on the floor and I was pacing around her.

"What am I supposed to do here, huh?" I asked. "You know, I've done what you're doing. I've said that shit you're saying and I know it's a lie."

"It's not a lie."

"It's a fucking lie." I almost kicked her coffee table.

"Maybe you lied to people, but I'm just trying to be honest," she said.

"Would you please stop saying that?"

"Listen, this has nothing to do with me," she said. "You don't love me." She was gesturing at the ground. "I could be any girl. This is about you. I can't just sit idly around here waiting for you to lose your fascination with the dowdy girl. You're right — it's not fun anymore. I really care about you, and you made me very happy . . ."

I wasn't listening to her. I was circling around her, like a rabid dog chained to a stake.

". . . but I can't hear myself think when you're in the room," she said. "Everything is a big game of pretend with you. 'Let's pretend to get married.' 'Let's pretend I'm gonna be a big country star.' "

I wanted to grab her and shake her. I felt like if I could hit something hard enough, I could will her to love me. I wanted her to cry.

" 'Just pretend you're someone else,' " she went on. "That's what you said to me in the club where I was singing that first night. Remember? Nothing is casual with you. Everything is a big deal."

"No, only you. Only you are a big deal," I said.

Her arms were now closed around her knees. I looked for something to hit. No way was some girl breaking up with me without crying.

She was cowering away from me, like she was worried I was going to hit her.

"For chrissakes, I'm not going to hit you." When I said that, it sounded like a threat. Sarah completely hid her face in her arms.

"I'm a great guy. You love me," I said. I didn't want to start crying. "Look at me. Would you please look at me?" The room was silent. "LOOK AT ME, I'M RIGHT HERE" I screamed, leaning down close to her.

She didn't look up. I stopped my pacing. The room was soundless.

"I'm handling this pretty badly, aren't I?" I said. "Listen, it'd mean a lot to me if you'd just look at me." I saw the clock in her kitchen. It read 12:03. "It's my birthday," I said. "I'm twenty-one."

She looked at me. Her face and eyes had taken on the appearance of a cadaver. I felt tears welling up. I knew I had to leave or I'd start sobbing.

"Okay. I'll go. . . . You'd like me to go, right?"

"Yes," she said, looking down again.

I picked up my presents. They were hard to carry. I looked around at the blue paint on the walls. I thought of the ovals I had drawn around her eyes when we'd painted the room.

I took a photograph of Sarah in my mind. She was tucked into a cramped ball in the center of the floor. One of her hands was constricting tightly around the knuckles of the other. Her face was hidden in her knees. Her black hair was draped around her legs. Her green shoes stuck out from underneath her brown dress. I tried to walk out of the room, but I couldn't.

"I'm sorry," I said, facing the opposite wall. "I want to make this easy on you. I don't want to be stupid, I really don't. But do you think you could just lie to me a little, or let me sleep here or something to make this a little easier?"

"I can't do that," she said.

"Yes, you can. I feel like you are playing some sick practical joke on me."

"I'm sorry you feel like that," she said.

"Would you talk to me like a person, please?"

"This happened to me before," she said, "and once I got through it, I was so grateful because I was much stronger."

"Strong? I am fucking strong." I stood up, grabbed the back of her refrigerator, and overturned it onto the floor.

She sat still and quiet. I stood above her looking at the mess I had made. My glasses were hanging crooked off my face. I straightened them.

"Where did you go?" I asked quietly.

She didn't answer.

"Yeah, well, I miss you," I said.

I gathered my presents and walked home.

SIXTEEN

The next day was my birthday. Hip hip hooray. Twenty-one years old and as manic as a three-legged wolf. I sat at a table across from my mother. We were in a restaurant called Mexico Magico. We liked to eat Mexican together, to pretend in some delusional way that we were still in Texas. I hated eating alone with my mother. I did it my whole life and it always made me feel like we were on a date.

My mother had on a gray suit. Her hair was light brown, and she'd recently given it streaks of blond. She'd taken the train in from Trenton, New Jersey. I don't know what it is, but most of the time, I can't look my mother in the eye. People always tell me how pretty she is — she's only seventeen years older than I am — but I try to never look.

"Do you have any Marlboros?" she asked.

My mother loves Marlboro cigarettes; any other brand is a sign of weakness. She told me that the first time she caught me smoking. I gave her one and lit it.

"So how's that girl?" she asked. I'd made the mistake of mentioning Sarah.

"She doesn't like me too much, Mom," I said, lighting a cigarette of my own.

"What's wrong with her?" she said, motioning to the waiter that we needed more chips and salsa. My mother and I have one identical problem: neither one of us can sit still.

"Nothing's wrong with her, Mom. She just doesn't like me."

I was looking around the restaurant, hoping my margarita would come soon. I'd wanted the waiter to card me, but he didn't.

"I always thought she sounded neurotic," my mother said. She has no trace of a southern accent.

"There's nothing neurotic about her." I was starting to get a sharp pain in my stomach.

Our drinks arrived, and my mother proceeded to take a napkin and wipe all the salt off the rim of her glass.

"Cheers," she said.

The waiters in the restaurant were all wearing sombreros. There was a guy in the back dressed in a black sequined vest, playing the mandolin. I didn't think any of them were Mexican; in fact, most of them looked Asian.

"You seem depressed," she said. "Are you okay?"

"Yeah. . . . I don't like birthdays."

"Nobody does," she said. "At a certain point, William, your father not calling you on your birthday becomes your problem, not his. He loves you very much. I'm sure of that. I think it just hurts him too much to remain in contact with you."

"I didn't expect him to call," I snapped. I didn't know what the hell she knew about it. The pain in my side was expanding. We sat listening to the mandolin. There was so much color in the room I was also developing a headache.

"Why do you think she doesn't like me?" I asked.

"Who? That girl?" my mother asked. "Because there's something wrong with her."

"No, Mom, something is wrong with me. What do you think it is?" I was really asking her.

"You respect people more who don't like you," she said. "That and you didn't go to college. Those are your only flaws."

Dropping out of college was the one thing that I'd ever done that truly disappointed my mother.

When I was a little kid, she was my greatest ally. Once, I went up to a boy in my art class and told him that his painting sucked. The teacher made me sit in the study hall and write a one-page essay on why I shouldn't use words like that. I wrote her that I had no idea "suck" was a bad word, that my mother dated lots of guys who used the word often to describe me. After she read the paper, my teacher hugged me with tears in her eyes.

When I got home my mother stonewalled me.

"You are incorrigible. I don't date 'lots' of guys, and I don't teach you to use words like 'SUCK.' "

I couldn't stop laughing.

"Why would you say that?" she asked.

"I was in trouble." I shrugged.

"Oh, so you use your poor old ma to get out of it."

"Uh-huh."

We both laughed.

"What did you tell her?" I asked.

"I told her to go to hell," my mother said.

Our food arrived. I sat there picking at my rice and beans. As always, I'd eaten too much chips and salsa. I wished that Sarah could have come to this dinner. I could've been removed and distant while they happily chatted. I wanted my childhood to be past tense, but I was having the sensation it was all happening again.

I listened to my mother talk about her new boyfriend, Harris. I felt what was sure to be an ulcer continuing to balloon in the depths of my stomach.

"He's very funny," she said. "I think I may be falling in love. You'll be astonished at how many times in your life you'll fall in love."

I hated myself. I hated my mother. I knew if I couldn't make it work with Sarah, I'd never be able to make it work with any woman. I thought I'd wind up some queer, whiny little mama's boy, masturbating in the corner. I wished that I had grown up with my father. It didn't seem like I knew the first thing about how men were supposed to behave. I thought there were certain qualities I lacked that should've been intrinsic. Something in me was perversely askew. One thing I was pretty sure about was men didn't sit around smoking cigarettes, drinking margaritas, getting all chatty with their moms.

There were these three men standing over at the bar glaring at me. They looked gay. I surveyed the room for a sexy woman.

I caught my mother focusing on me with a silly grin on her face.

"What?" I asked.

"I don't know — you just look so different. Older," she said.

"Give it a break, would ya, Mom?" I said, taking out a cigarette. I gave her one as well. She said she only smoked when she was around me.

The guys standing across from us were starting to make my

skin crawl. I wanted to stand up and tell them to stop goggling at me. I also wanted to run away. I wondered what insane people felt like.

"Hey, how come I'm not baptized?" I asked my mother.

"What?" she asked.

"I don't know — weren't you the least bit concerned with the state of my soul?"

"Believe me, William, there was nothing anyone at Fort Worth First Methodist was going to do for your soul."

"I don't know why I asked," I said. "It's not important."

I was beginning to get worried that maybe I didn't have a soul. Sarah had accused me of pretending. She was right. My mother and I were always pretending. I was pretending to be a Texan and she was pretending she wasn't. I remembered the candlelight dinners we used to have every Sunday night, no matter where we lived. I thought of the time I pretended to be the abused neighbor kid to help her out of an unpleasant date.

"You've been ignoring me since you were fifteen," she said, "and I was thinking that a good birthday resolution might be to change your attitude toward your poor old ma."

I didn't answer her. My mother was into resolutions.

"Don't be so moody," my mother said, taking a drag from her cigarette. She loved smoking — that was obvious. "A lot of bad things are going to happen to you. First off, you're going to die. So, that said, there's not much to worry about. No matter what else happens, you really only have two options: you can either handle things well and be happy, or you can handle them poorly and be miserable."

I finally looked her in the eye. She was a bewitching woman. There was a luminous glow about her face. Her skin appeared to reflect light. She was still difficult to look at. It was something in the corners of her eyes; no matter where she was or what she was doing — holding a glass of champagne at a New Year's Eve party in Baton Rouge, waiting tables in a chandelier-laden New Hampshire hotel, watching me from the back of a New York City theater — she looked lost. Somewhere along the line, she'd been completely misplaced. That always made me embarrassingly sad.

"Look, William, I'm disappointed. I can't tell you that I'm not. I thought my life was going to be so much more interesting than it's turned out. But what am I going to do about it?" She raised her shoulders and smiled at me.

No matter where I went, everything was making me want to cry.

She gave me a couple of button-down oxford cloth shirts and told me she hoped I would wear them. She made me take the wrapping paper off neatly so that she could use it again. I kissed her good-bye. She said that she wished I'd take better care of myself and that she loved me. All I could manage was "Thanks."

When I left Mexico Magico, I was scared, truly afraid, for what seemed like the first time in my life. Taking slow, meticulous steps, I ventured down Eighth Avenue, past the transvestites looming around Port Authority, past the madness of hockey fans cheering their way out of Madison Square Garden, and back down into the freaks and wanna-be freaks of Greenwich Village. I didn't know which group I fell into, but they both sounded bad.

SEVENTEEN

Samantha was wearing tight black Levi's and a pink angora sweater that showed off what remarkable tits she had. They weren't saggy like Sarah's. She had sexy little hips, too. She liked it when I would rest my hand on the top of her ass as we walked. She said it made her feel sexy.

She was about to be the third girl I'd slept with in two weeks. There were no lamp shades on any of my lights and the lightbulbs glared. Earlier that night at dinner we'd put away three bottles of wine, so we were both pretty sauced. I'd listened to her tell me every silly thing that had happened to her since I last saw her, looking straight into her eyes. Samantha loves that. She loves being taken seriously.

I was starting to want her to leave — either that or to just start screwing around. I sat down in my chair.

"You should really put your CDs back in their cases," she said, riffling through my collection.

"Yeah, I guess," I said.

"What was her name again?"

"Who?" I asked. Sarah was not a subject I wanted to take up.

"The girl you were going out with? The crunchy one."

"Sarah," I said.

"Didn't seem like your type," Samantha said. She assumed anyone remotely unlike herself was not my type.

Sam moved around the room. She noticed the lipstick on a cigarette filter in an ashtray. She noticed that I had my blankets laid out on the couch. She noticed everything. I was sitting there in my chair trying not to lose consciousness.

"I heard she wasn't fucking you," she said.

"That's not true. We had sex," I said. Samantha was interested in the details of everything.

"I didn't believe it when I heard it. I couldn't imagine you not screwing anybody."

"She wouldn't sleep with me for a while," I said in my own defense.

"Why not? She have some kind of hangup?"

I didn't want to talk about Sarah. She was all I thought about, but I didn't want to get started. Being this drunk was the best I'd felt all day. I hated waking up in the mornings. I didn't have anything to do, and if I did, I blew it off. I was having a peculiar problem. It'd start seconds after I woke up. The word "faggot" would pound through my brain in steady sync with my pulse. I couldn't stop it. I'd have trouble even thinking in complete sentences. Standing in the shower, the voice would boom in my head. I'd slam the back of my skull against the tile. That'd work for a minute. I'd try to remind myself of things I used to think about before I met Sarah. I wanted to know how I was supposed to occupy my brain for all the idle minutes of the day. The Dallas Cowboys. I'd force myself to think about them. Roger Staubach, Danny White, Tony Dorsett. I'd sift through all their great games. Then slowly I'd hear it again, my own voice, steadily pumping, keeping perfect time, calling me faggot. It wouldn't stop all day, until I was hopelessly drunk. Then my brain would settle again.

I stood up and walked over to Samantha. I walked slowly because I didn't want to fall over. I tried to gaze at her the way I imagined other people would before they kissed someone.

"What happened to your phone?" she asked, pointing to the pile of twisted electronics next to my answering machine.

"I broke it."

"Why?" Samantha didn't feel like making out.

I took off my glasses and set them down. I didn't have the energy to put in my contacts at all anymore. I rubbed my temples. My mind was doing cartwheels.

"Because I was in love with her," I slurred.

"You were in love with Sarah?"

"Yeah."

"No, you weren't." She was staring at me. I couldn't see her at all.

"Maybe. Who knows?" I said, walking back to my chair. I didn't want to come off as too drunk, because then Samantha definitely wouldn't sleep with me. She likes to at least be able to pretend to herself that when we have sex, there's something a little personal going on.

"What do you do if you want to make a phone call?" she asked.

"I bought another phone. I just haven't wanted to make any calls."

"You called me?" she asked.

"From the street," I answered.

"And Sarah doesn't love you back?" Samantha was getting serious. It was making me uncomfortable.

"No," I said.

Samantha eased herself over, moved the blankets and some other crap off the couch, and sat down across from me.

"Are you sad?" she asked. Her eyes were generous, interested, and caring.

"Whatever," I said. I really couldn't bear how sentimental she was getting.

"What happened?" she asked.

"Sarah told me she didn't want to see me anymore, so I ran over to her house and recited Romeo's soliloquy outside her window, and when I came home she had left a message saying that if I hung around her apartment anymore she'd call the cops." That was one of the things I didn't want to be talking about. It sounded tragic.

I'd gone over to Sarah's apartment building a week before and stood out on the street again, fixating on the light in her window. There was someone else there, a woman. I imagined that they were talking about me. "What were you *thinking?*" her friend would ask. "I don't *know,*" Sarah would say, trying not to laugh.

I wanted her to remember me. I didn't want to go out whining. I wanted her to see that she was the one losing, not me. I didn't want to be weak anymore. I stood there in the middle of Ninth Street at two o'clock in the morning and commenced with my plan.

"WHAT LIGHT THROUGH YONDER WINDOW BREAKS? IT IS THE EAST, AND JULIET IS THE SUN. ARISE, FAIR SUN, AND KILL THE ENVIOUS MOON." Nervous adrenaline was reeling through my body.

Her friend came over to the window, looked out, turned

back, and said something to Sarah. Lots of other people started opening windows and peering out as well.

"THAT THOU HER MAID ART FAR MORE FAIR THAN SHE: BE NOT HER MAID, SINCE SHE IS ENVIOUS; HER VESTAL LIVERY IS BUT SICK AND GREEN AND NONE BUT FOOLS DO WEAR IT."

I really hit that last line. Sarah came over to the window. I was in a state of terror, but I couldn't stop.

"IT IS MY LADY, O, IT IS MY LOVE." I pointed at Sarah. "O, THAT SHE KNEW SHE WERE." Dead leaves were piled in the gutters. I kicked at them.

Sarah touched her friend's shoulder and they both left the window. I couldn't see them anymore but I didn't care. I was feeling better.

"SEE, HOW SHE LEANS HER CHEEK UPON HER HAND! O, THAT I WERE A GLOVE UPON THAT HAND, THAT I MIGHT TOUCH THAT CHEEK!"

I was hoping that I was accidentally describing her position with perfect accuracy.

"O, SPEAK AGAIN, BRIGHT ANGEL!" I called out. I knew more but I felt like that was a good place to stop. Some people were deriding me with catcalls, shrieking for me to shut the fuck up, but I distinctly heard one person clapping.

"HEY, SARAH! HEY, SARAH!" I shouted.

She didn't come to the window.

"YOU CAN'T SAY I DIDN'T GO OUT WITH A BANG. YOU CAN'T SAY THAT."

I walked away. I was feeling the best I'd felt since I'd been back from Paris. She'd always remember that, I thought. I walked home beaming with pride.

When I arrived, there was a message.

"Uh . . . William," she said, her voice shaking, "if you want to talk to me, this is not how to do it. I'm scared to leave my apartment. Please don't come by anymore. . . . Bye."

I called her back.

"I didn't mean to scare you," I said. "I just wanted to say good-bye with the best words I know."

"Good-bye," she said and hung up. I hung up the phone and with both hands slammed it against the wall. The receiver broke into three pieces and the buttons popped out of the base.

"What a bitch," Samantha said, sitting on my couch. She had one leg draped over the other in a sexy way. Her jeans were tight around the curves of her ass. "If anyone did that outside my window, my heart would break in two," she said.

"Yeah?" I asked, seeing my opening. I knew we'd better start fooling around soon or I wasn't going to be able to go through with it. Carefully, I walked over to the couch and kissed her. For an instant I thought about telling her I loved her, but I knew she'd take me seriously. I kissed her neck and the tops of her breasts. I tried to go slow. Samantha gets standoffish if she thinks all you want to do is screw her.

"Have you heard from her since then?" she asked, moving me away from her. One of Sam's considerable problems was that she consistently spoke about two decibels too loud.

"No." I tried to gracefully unbutton her jeans.

"Let's go to the bed," she said, reaching for my hand.

"I don't have a bed," I said.

"What do you mean?"

"I hucked it out the window," I said. I didn't want to be

talking about that either. That happened the night of the *Romeo and Juliet* fiasco.

"Why?" Samantha asked. She stopped fooling around entirely, and moved away from me.

"I didn't like it anymore." Without my glasses, I couldn't make out the details of her face at all.

"Oh, my God," Samantha said. She was apparently moved by my instability. She returned to the couch and kissed me on the lips. Then she slunk around the room with her jeans still unbuttoned. Samantha turned off all the lights. I wanted to run away. I hunkered down on my couch, feeling like an eight-year-old boy. Everything made me feel like an eight-year-old boy. The problem was that I knew that I wasn't.

I started kissing her. I started pulling down her pants. I buried my face in her breasts. She unzipped my pants and kicked the whole thing off by starting to give me a blow job. When she did that I couldn't tell if she was a guy or a girl. I pulled her up. I kissed her eyes, her cheeks, her teeth. I smelled her hair. I caressed her whole body. Samantha wanted to have sex. She wasn't doing me any goddamn favors. She didn't want to talk about it. I hated Sarah. I turned Samantha around, pulled her underwear to her knees and started having sex with her.

"Do you have any condoms?" she asked. I always thought that was a stupid way of saying "rubbers," even when Sarah said it. It was trying to make them sound nice or something.

"Yeah, yeah . . . hold on a minute." I stood up and ran to the bathroom. I tried to go fast because I didn't want to lose my hard-on. I knew if I lost it, it wasn't coming back, and I wasn't sure if I could handle that dilemma again. With the lights out and my glasses off I couldn't see a damn thing. I turned on the

ETHAN HAWKE

bathroom light and looked for the condoms. They were right
next to Sarah's tampons. I couldn't believe that was the one
thing she left me. I liked them there, though. If people came
in, I thought, they'd see them and think that I still had a girlfriend.

I took the condom out, and struggled to put it on. It was
about halfway on before I gave up. I threw it into the toilet
and zipped up my pants. I stumbled back out into the living
room. I was definitely nauseous. My mouth was spontaneously filling with saliva. Samantha was still on her knees
with her ass floating above the couch. Her head was resting
on a pillow.

"You gotta go," I said. I wanted to be more pleasant about
it, but I didn't know how. I walked over to her, picked up her
underwear and handed it to her.

"What are you talking about?" she asked.

"I hate condoms," I said.

"Don't worry about it," she said gently.

"You don't want to be here right now," I said.

"Yes, I do." She was trying to be all sensitive again. I felt
around for my glasses. I thought they might give me more of
an appearance of being sane. I put them on.

She was standing in front of me naked. Samantha's not shy
at all. She's very beautiful. I felt terrible. I couldn't figure out
why she was always so damn kind. I sort of wanted to hurt her,
take her face and do something mean to it.

"Listen, Sam, do me a favor and go. I can't deal with anybody right now. I'll call you tomorrow."

"I want to talk to you." She reached out and touched my
face. I flinched.

"I'll call you tomorrow," I said again.

146

We stood there taking each other in. She was still naked. "I really just want to be alone," I said.

"Oh, my God," she said and abruptly put on her clothes, picked up her bag, and left without closing the door.

As soon as she left, I wished that she hadn't. I wanted to chase after her and tell her I was sorry. I was sorry about so many things. It seemed to me that I'd revealed the best part of myself to Sarah, and somehow she still had it.

I shut the door and walked back into the bathroom. I studied myself in the mirror. I was wearing my gray sweater. My eyes looked like they were bleeding underneath my glasses. I hadn't shaved in weeks. I had many more whiskers on the left side of my face than on the right. I wondered if that meant anything. I had my father's mouth and I was beginning to get a very distant look in my eyes that I remembered him having.

The last time I saw him, I was seven years old. We were in the DFW airport on Christmas Day. I had a guitar case loaded with toy guns. The airport people wouldn't let me board the plane with it. I was forced to say good-bye to him right there by the metal detectors.

"I'll make sure this gets on the plane," he said. "And if it doesn't, I'll just mail it to you."

"Okay," I said. There was a woman from the airline dressed entirely in red waiting for me on the other side of the detector.

"I promise you'll get it," my father said, leaning down to me with the guitar case still in his hand.

"That'd be good," I said.

"The Cowboys play again on Sunday, so don't miss it."

"I won't." I loved the Cowboys.

"This is our year," my father said smiling.

147

"I know." I didn't feel like talking. I didn't want to go back to my mom.

"All right, William, you take care. We love you," he said. I wondered who "we" was, but then I remembered his new wife. She was standing right behind him. He liked her a lot.

"Never stray too far from Texas in your heart," he said, thumping me on the chest. That always seemed to me a rather poetic thing for a management consultant to say.

We hugged. I walked through the metal detector and the red lady from the airline led me to my gate. She insisted on holding my hand. That pissed me off. I didn't think I needed to be walked anywhere. I could read the signs. I turned around and saw my father waving to me with my guitar case in one hand and his new wife in the other.

I thought about calling my father and telling him that I hadn't ever strayed too far from Texas in my heart and what a crock of shit that advice was.

I went into the kitchen and poured myself a glass of water. As I bent down to the sink, I bumped my head on one of the kitchen cabinet doors. I started pounding the shit out of it with my fist. I punched it over and over until my knuckles burst open. Then I ripped it off the wall. Then I ripped the next one off. My hand was killing me. I wanted to break it. I wanted to have a cast around it, so people would ask, "What happened?" and I'd say, "See how strong I am? I broke my own hand."

I went into the bathroom to clean up. I was breathing heavy but I wasn't crying. Blood was dripping everywhere. My own face was gawking at me in the mirror. I took a deep breath, contorted my mouth, and prepared to hit the glass. I stopped. I didn't want to cry. I slowly swung my fist and rested my bleeding hand on my reflection.

I suddenly wanted to talk to my father. I didn't care how late it was. I wanted to call him and tell him that he was a Benedict Arnold. I was furious that he'd never asked me to come live with him. I thought maybe as soon as I told him to go to hell, I'd feel better.

I didn't have his number. I'd have to call my mother to get it. I was positive she still had it.

I went back into the kitchen, stepped over all the broken cabinet doors on the ground, and unwrapped the phone that I'd bought a few days before. I untwisted the wires with my good hand. Blood was spilling all over the white walls and the wood floors. Giant flakes of dead, white skin were hanging off my knuckles.

I plugged the phone into the wall and dug around for my mother's number. She changed addresses so often it was impossible to keep track.

Her boyfriend answered in a sleepy voice. I rammed the receiver down with my left hand. Then gently, I set it back in its place. I didn't want to break another phone. If I did that, I wouldn't be able to call anybody.

My right hand was hanging limp in the air. Before I could think about what I was doing, I crammed the receiver back under my neck and started dialing Sarah's number with my left hand.

If I got her machine, I'd hang up. If she answered, I'd apologize for calling so late and tell her that I was losing my mind. I got her machine but I couldn't hang up. Her voice on the message sounded so friendly.

"Hey, listen, it's me . . . William," I said. The pain in my hand was so intense, it took my breath away. "Are you there? . . . Are you there?" I asked. "Ah . . . Okay. Sorry for calling so late. Give me a call when you get a chance. Happy Thanksgiving." I figured she wasn't home. On the way back from Little Italy, I'd walked Samantha by Sarah's place, and noticed that the light was out. I figured Sarah wouldn't be angry if she saw me outside her window with another girl. It wouldn't be like I was harassing her. Besides, Samantha was better looking than Sarah, and I wanted her to see me having such a good time.

When I hung up, I called right back. It was wonderful to listen to her soft, calm voice on the message again.

"Hey, sorry for leaving another message. I just wanted to tell you that I know you might not want to talk to me, and if that's the case, don't worry about it. We'll talk when the time is right. See ya." I hung up. I was pleased with that message. I was trying to sound sane and rational. I thought, that way she'd be more likely to call back.

Except that then I realized if I gave her an excuse, she'd never call me back. I called her again immediately.

"Hey, listen, it's me again. This is pretty absurd, huh?" I was still seated on the kitchen floor with all the broken cabinet doors lying around me and the bright kitchen light glaring above me. "I just know that you're not going to call me back and you should. I mean, I'd like you to, that'd be nice. Not that you give a rat's ass about being nice, because I know you don't." I was eyeballing the bare lightbulb above me, allowing my retinas to burn. "It's just that I went out with this other girl tonight, Samantha — remember her? I mean, I know that you don't like her because she doesn't spout out a lot of intellectual bullshit, but she's real smart. You shouldn't think that just because a girl's pretty she's not smart, because that's not the case. I don't know, it always seemed to me that you had a lot of hangups about shit like that." I was starting to get tired. I was still concerned I might throw up.

"Maybe it's just that you try to be, like, all extra smart because you're not pretty. But you shouldn't do that, because I think you're pretty. Not that you're, like, fantastically interested in receiving emotional advice from me or anything but — Samantha's definitely an attractive woman, and she's smart, and we had a good time." I knew I was babbling but I couldn't bear the idea of hanging up.

"It gave me some distance on us, you know? It made me miss you less. Not like I'm some kind of maniac missing you or something, so don't go getting all freaked out and call the cops. Just call me back, that'd be cool, you know? I mean, I'm aware that I'm not first on your list of people to please right now, but . . . ah . . . give me a call . . . I really need to talk to somebody." I took a long pause, and looked around the kitchen. I couldn't see anything except five or six different doubles of the overhead lightbulb blazing in my eyes.

"You know what I was thinking the other day? Remember how you used to want to walk on the curb and have me walk on the street so that we could be the same height? Yeah, well, that's really fucked up. You shouldn't do that. I'm taller than you, and you should just face it. . . . Yeah, well . . . listen, I don't want to hang up, because I know as soon as I do, I'm going to feel like a real moron. So please call me back, otherwise I'll probably kill myself or something — I'M NOT GOING TO KILL MYSELF. You know, you really have no sense of humor whatsoever. That always drove me crazy about you. All

right, so call me, okay? . . . I'm going to hang up now. . . .
Bye." I hung up the phone and closed my eyes. I decided I
had to call her one more time and tell her I was deeply apolo-
getic for calling in the first place.

Only this time she picked up the phone.

"William, you have to stop calling me," she said, point-
blank.

I lost my breath. I was instantaneously humiliated.

"I thought you were probably at your mom's for Thanksgiving," I eventually said.

"It's now three-thirty-eight on Sunday morning. Thanksgiving was on Thursday."

"Oh, yeah," I said. "I remember."

There was a long silence.

"Well, I just wanted to call you back," I said, "and tell you I
was sorry for calling. I'm pretty drunk right now."

"Why don't you go to sleep?" she said. It made me so happy
to hear her speak in the least bit compassionately.

"I can't sleep," I said. "I've been thinking about you a lot recently and I was —"

"William, I appreciate that you're thinking about me, but
we shouldn't talk now, not for a long time."

"Yeah, I think you're right," I said. I wanted to agree on
anything.

"Okay, good-bye," she said, and hung up. I continued to
hold the phone with my shoulder pressed up to my ear until the
nagging sound of the dial tone started drumming in my ear.

With my left hand I battered the phone into the floor
repetitively until all of its buttons, screws, and wires popped
out and slid across the wood panels. That'd been my third
phone in three weeks.

The silence in my room was overpowering.

Then it started again, like a metronome, in perfect syncopation with the blood throbbing in my temples, the voice: "Faggot."

I tried to stand up, but my crippled hand screwed up my balance. I slipped in the blood on the kitchen floor. Finally I wandered out through the living room and back into the bathroom. I leaned over and stuck my face into the commode. The condom was still floating in the water. I stood up and looked at myself in the mirror again. I'd somehow gotten blood all over everything — my face, my hair, my neck. I saw myself wearing Sarah's dress. I could see the detailed green-floral print, the shoulder straps; it looked like I had breasts.

The silence amplified itself to a screech. "Faggot, faggot" the voice hammered in my head.

I stumbled and tripped my way into the bedroom. There was no bed anymore so the floor was empty. There were lines of dust around where the edge of the mattress had been. The floor was gently rocking back and forth as if it were being carried by waves. I looked up at the ceiling and waited for the motion to stop. Slowly the teetering eased itself down, and the screeching in my head became simply the dull hum of silence. I looked around the room, noticing little things like paper clips and broken pencils and unlabeled cassette tapes spread out along the floor; tiny little things I didn't even remember losing. I could see out the window. It looked as if there were only three or four lights left on in the entire city. I moved slowly, picked up a T-shirt, wrapped it around my hand, and I knelt down on the floor. I'm not Catholic or anything but I decided to pray.

EIGHTEEN

"Oh, Christ" was the first thing Samantha said when I showed up at her dorm room the next morning.

She escorted me over to the university infirmary and by the time an intern had finished applying my seventeen stitches, the previous evening's disaster had seemingly been forgiven. That was the nature of our relationship and always had been.

The first time I ever had sex was with Samantha in Wendy Engelhardt's parents' bedroom. Wendy was throwing a keg party. Samantha and I snuck upstairs past where we had been expressly forbidden to go and commenced with our plan. For the occasion, Sam wore a purple lace bra with matching panties and garters. She was sixteen. She said she wanted to look pretty. I told her she did. Cautious not to mess up Wendy's parents' sheets, we lay down on top of the comforter. I was so nervous I could barely touch her except in harsh, bold movements. Wrestling our way around the bed, we arrived at the correct position. I was lying on top of her, in between her legs. I knew I had a rubber in my jeans pocket down on the floor. I looked down at Samantha.

"Do you love me?" she whispered in her most sultry voice. "Will you love me forever? Will you make me so happy for the rest of my life? Will you take me away and make me your wife?" She gave me a devious smirk.

She was quoting from a Meat Loaf song we both liked. I kissed her and with the brute force of a Sherman tank drove myself inside her.

After I came, we just lay there listening to the muted sounds of the party below us. Neither one of us had any idea of what to say to the other. I asked her if she enjoyed it. She said that it hurt but it was nice anyway.

A buddy of mine knocked on the door and called out, asking me if I'd come play quarters. I looked at Samantha to ask if it was all right. She smiled.

"Are you sure?" I asked.

"If you want to," she said.

"I'll be right back." I jumped off the bed, put my clothes on, and ran downstairs, leaving her alone. I drank a few beers and told my friends that I'd just lost my virginity. I'd always felt pretty shitty about that night. It was the first time either one of us had had sex and the first time she got pregnant.

Somehow I'd agreed to spend Christmas Eve with Sam, mostly to avoid seeing my mother. We were sitting in Wolf's Diner near St. Patrick's Cathedral, waiting for midnight Mass to start. I was wearing an old, brown corduroy jacket with red flannel lining, a pair of tired, green wool pants, and a black cashmere sweater that belonged to Samantha. Sam was all decked out in a sleek dress that fit her like a sheath. Her hair was stretched tightly back across her head. My right hand still had some stitches in it. I'd missed my appointment to get them removed and was just slowly picking them out myself. Recently, I'd been unable to look a single person in the eye and was averaging about a hundred trips to the bathroom a day. The brief moments of watching Samantha's breasts sway as she spoke were my only occasions of solace.

"I went to a fortune teller a couple of days ago," she said. "This little old gypsy lady up on One Hundred Twenty-Eighth Street. And do you know what the first thing she asked me was?" Samantha spoke a fraction too loud even when she was trying to be serious. I didn't respond to her question. I was pulling on my teeth. They hurt. Something about my mouth wasn't closing properly.

"As soon as I walked in and sat down, she asked me what happened to my children." Samantha's eyes were filling with water. I didn't want her to cry. She did it all the time but still it pissed me off. I was so emotionally brittle I couldn't withstand any demonstration of feeling.

"I told her that I didn't have any children," she continued, "and this gypsy woman said, 'No, of course not, they're dead.'" Samantha paused, tears hanging on her lashes.

"I told her about the abortions, and she said that she could see the spirits of our two children floating above me. It gave me the heebie-jeebies," she said. Two tears fell from one eye. She quickly wiped them away. It was amazing how giant Samantha's tears were. Each one was a round and sculpted teardrop, straight out of a forties movie.

"I mean, no shit, can you imagine?" she said. Sam was trying hard not to be oversentimental. "I go in there to, like, find out whether or not I should keep bothering with you. Or if I'm going to get A's on my exams, junk like that, right? And she tells me I have two dead children following me around."

I didn't say anything. I knew I was supposed to but I just couldn't think of a damn thing to say. This was the last conversation I wanted to have. I looked around the diner. There were families all dressed up in their Christmas best.

"When you broke my heart I was sad for a long time," Samantha said, dabbing her eyes with a paper napkin.

"I'm sorry," I said.

"Good," she smiled.

We sat in silence. The diner was noisy. The waiters were scurrying around handing out large, weighty plates of turkey and mashed potatoes. We were only drinking coffee. Lately I'd been eating all my meals at a fast-food dive on First Avenue called Burritoville. I started yanking at my teeth again.

"I wish you'd talk," Samantha said.

I shrugged my shoulders.

"I mean, don't you think it's odd what that lady said to me?"

"Yeah," I said, nodding slowly. I poured some salt out on the table and tried to balance the glass shaker on one of its flat edges. Samantha watched me.

"I wish you'd stop doing that," she said.

I set the salt shaker down and blew the salt off the table. Most of it accidentally landed on her lap.

"William?" Samantha said, smiling. "You really don't love me at all, do you?" Her mascara was smudged around her eyes. She looked very dramatic.

"I don't know," I said.

"It's pretty screwy, you know? Because, I'm, like, a feminist and all that. I mean, I am. I want to be my own person and have my own life. I'm going to college and all that jazz, but I see you and I want to take care of you. I'd stay home and sand the floors for you, you know? Stupid shit like that. I mean, if you did actually want to have a baby, I'd do it. I mean, I'd like to do it."

I was quiet. I didn't know why she was doing this. She glared at me, looking for a response, and then turned away. I knew she'd get hostile soon.

"You're the most selfish person I've ever met," she said.

I nodded slowly.

"If Sarah called tomorrow, would you go back out with her?" She was waiting for me to speak. I wished she hadn't said Sarah's name out loud.

"She won't call." I looked up and gave Sam a phony smile. I wanted to be nice, I really did. I missed Sarah the way an amputee might miss his legs. I wanted to speak with her. I wanted to spend Christmas with her and her mother. I wondered if they were going to church tonight. I wondered if St. Patrick's would be anything like Notre-Dame.

It wasn't. It was beautiful and had loads of stained glass and sculptures of apostles and crap like that but it didn't have any dignity. There were two rows of thick stone columns leading from the front doors to the altar, with a television screen mounted on each one. The screens were all focused on a life-size model of the Nativity scene. Entering the church, all we could see were rows and rows of small television sets featuring the same fairy-tale image. It was like a Christian hall of mirrors. Somehow the birth of Christ had the guise of a game show.

I held Samantha's hand, focused my eyes on her hips, and let her lead us, slithering our way through the thousands of people all looking for a seat.

When we found a place, we took off our coats and sat down. We hadn't spoken to one another since we left the diner. It was too cold outside to talk. Inside the church, everyone was chatting enthusiastically. I looked over at Sam and she burst into sobs. Her shoulders shook violently. I grabbed her and kissed the tears right off her face. Then we started blatantly making out. Samantha was wearing a white satin dress that was embroidered with cream lace. She was ravishing. The mascara was streaming from the corners of her eyes, and it made her look like a little girl who had experimented with her mother's makeup. All of a sudden I was crazy about her. I reached my hand up her dress. Churches always make me feel sexy.

"Stop," she whispered. Then she kissed me soft on the cheek. Her face was sopping wet. She was really outrageously gorgeous. She opened up her purse and pulled out an old pile of paper napkins and wiped her makeup off my face first and then off her own.

"Let's get outta here," I said.

Samantha didn't respond. She was holding a small mirror and reapplying her makeup.

The service hadn't even started yet and already I was worried I wasn't going to make it. I wished I'd gone to the can before I left the diner.

Samantha nodded politely at all the faces moving in around us. I couldn't find a comfortable position on the pew. My wallet was digging into my ass.

Loud bells started clamoring everywhere. The congregation fell instantaneously silent.

"The Lord be with you," someone announced.

"And also with you," the entire church echoed back.

It was horrible. I was nervous like a cat. We had to keep standing up and sitting down again. I'd been hoping to maybe

finally get some sleep, but with all the carrying on, it was fu-
tile.

When it was time to sing, Samantha offered me the hymnal. There was no way I was going to sing. I let my hand hang
down loose and casually allowed it to bump against her bottom. I wanted to get down to some heavy petting right there
in the church. I could feel hundreds of eyes pressing behind
me. If I couldn't disappear, I wanted to offend them. I wondered what everyone would do if I just started pissing right
there on the floor.

The priest stepped up to the pulpit and began to speak. His
nasty little wrinkle-ridden face appeared on all ten thousand
video screens. There was no way to avoid his pompous stare.
I fixated my eyes on Samantha's knees. I couldn't look at him.
I couldn't look at any men.

Samantha's best quality was that from no angle did she look
like a man.

I was terrified of men.

"Don't be afraid to be innocent," were the first words the
priest spoke. His voice boomed over the church sound sys-
tem.

I didn't think churches should have sound systems.

Samantha started gently tracing different patterns across
my thigh with her finger. I tried to kiss her. There were too
many people around us; even Sam was getting shy. I was hun-
gry for her. The pew shook slightly to the rhythm of the
priest's voice. Samantha unfastened the first button of my
pants and tickled my stomach. I quickly undid a few more
buttons. She snuggled up close to me and eased her hand inside my pants. I held her tight and kissed her ear. She giggled.

There was a man dressed entirely in New York Giants paraphernalia sitting at the end of our aisle in a wheelchair. He was drooling and didn't have any control over his arms, but he was ecstatic. Somehow the words and the music, or maybe it was all the people, filled him with joy. I thought he should have been delivering the sermon.

The priest was talking about brotherhood and a maple tree. I didn't understand the relevance, but somehow all people of the world were like the leaves of a maple tree, each one uniquely different but always undeniably a maple leaf. My father used to play the *Maple Leaf Rag* on the piano. I would've rather listened to that.

Then the priest just went off with words like "sin," "deviance," "hatred," "ignorance," "lies," "deceit," "evil," "jealousy," "fear." I tried not to listen and just concentrate on how good Samantha's hand felt down my pants.

"Don't be afraid of compassion," was his closing statement. There was a murmur of approval from the crowd, but I was hard-pressed to figure out how it was all supposed to correlate with the first Noel. I was just irritated we had to sing again.

Sam removed her hand, picked up the hymnal and motioned for me to stand up. Samantha didn't understand anything. I couldn't stand up. I had a hard-on.

Before I could take in what was happening, everyone in the church spontaneously turned to one another, saying "Peace" and joyously shaking hands. To me it was like a forest going up in flames. I quickly refastened my pants, grabbed Samantha's hand and dragged her out down the aisle.

"What's the matter?" she said.

"Let's just get out of here," I said. "I think I'm gonna die."

I plowed our way in between the people. At the end of our

row, I came face-to-face with the man in the wheelchair. He reached out and grabbed my arm with a viselike grip. He was smiling widely and one of his eyes was rolling. I looked down at him.

"Peace," he said.

Outside, a few sparse snowflakes were beginning to fall. The cold air stung my face and eyes. When Sam stepped out from the heavy church doors she was livid. Poised on top of the front steps, she cocked her head at me. Her face and her arms were turning a blotchy red from the ice in the air. In one hand she held her purse, dangling limp at her side. In the other, she held her coat. I wished she'd put it on.

I stood a few steps below her.

"You gotta understand one thing," I said. "For about three and a half minutes, I believed in destiny. And that, you know, I had one." My voice was raw and cracking like an old man's, and my hands were freezing into tight fists.

"You know something, William?" she asked. She was shivering. "I've spent so much time thinking you were secretly a good person, and you're not." She turned her head up to the sky and put on her overcoat.

"I hope you know I won't sleep with you tonight," she said, adjusting her collar up around her ears. She took a step down toward the street, but, in her heels, she slipped on a patch of ice.

I offered her my arm. She accepted and we walked down the front steps of St. Patrick's Cathedral. There were still a few stragglers rushing past us, in a hopeful attempt to catch the last few minutes of the service.

We walked up Sixth Avenue. We passed some hookers. I couldn't believe there were hookers out on Christmas Eve.

Finally it was too cold and we hailed a taxi. Samantha bent down and slid inside the cab.

"Are you coming?" she asked.

We filed through her doorway, and Sam put on a nightgown and went to bed. I didn't know how girls always thought of things like putting on nightgowns. I watched TV. I didn't think they should air television on Christmas. I turned the channels fast. Samantha had cable. She would. Sarah didn't even have a television.

In Texas, when I knew the Christmas Eve service was over, I would ask my father, "How much longer, Dad?"

"It just ended," he'd say. "You were fantastic. Quiet the whole time."

I thought maybe I should call my father and tell him Merry Christmas. Instead, I took off my shirt and laid myself down on Samantha's bed. I couldn't tell if she was asleep or not. Her radiator was hissing and clunking.

Finally I closed my eyes and fell out of consciousness.

I woke up sobbing. The sun was up again. There was a light dusting of snow outside the window. The room smelled old and stale.

"What happened?" she asked.

"I had a fuckin' nightmare," I said.

I was having those weird half-convulsions on her chest.

We walked out onto Amsterdam Avenue together and Samantha flagged down a cab. I didn't know where she was headed.

The roads were icy and traffic was slow. Before she stepped in, she said, "Don't call me."

When she shut the taxi door, she rolled down the window and looked up at me.

"Merry Christmas," she said, not smiling.

I thought it was time to go home.

NINETEEN

I loved trains. I loved anything that moved. I sat down on the neon-blue plastic seats of the New Jersey Transit train and let it carry me. My eyes burned from the white glare outside the window and from the withered contacts in my eyes. The meadowlands were dusted with ice. I could see the wind crossing the terrain, stirring up the snow into small tumble-weed shapes and then whisking up to the sky in twisted patterns of concentric circles. All I wanted was some rest.

I'd left Samantha's and gone straight to Penn Station. The place was in chaos. There were hundreds of families waiting for trains, standing around with shopping bags heaped with presents. The floor was one long puddle of filthy melting snow. I'd called my mom from a pay phone. Electronic Christmas music tinkled through the overhead speakers. I figured it was designed to numb the masses. It was driving me insane.

My mom was appropriately thrilled that I was coming home. She warned me that Harris and his family were over and asked what I was wearing. I looked down at my grimy corduroy jacket and the green pants I'd slept in. I told her I was in an Armani suit. She asked that I please at least comb my hair.

There was a black guy sitting next to me on the train buried in a humongous, blue down jacket and listening to a Walkman. He was close to my age. I could hear loud, driving music pummeling his ears. He and I were the only ones not carrying any luggage. We didn't speak the entire hour and fifteen minutes it took us to travel into Trenton.

I thought of the first Christmas after my parents were separated. I was three and my mother was twenty. She woke me up well before the sun rose. I was anxious out of my mind, thinking it was time for presents. She asked me to put on my shoes and a jacket and told me not to worry about pants. She said my pajamas would be fine.

I could hear my mother's monster red Pontiac warming up outside.

"Where we going?" I asked her. She didn't answer.

My mother was talking to herself as she drove. She kept repeating my father's name over and over as if he were in the car. I didn't say anything. We circled the city of Fort Worth at least twice. It was Christmas morning, so there wasn't any traffic. When we returned home, my father was standing in the driveway wearing a blue jeans jacket. My mother told me to stay in the car.

"You said you wouldn't be here," I heard her say as she slammed the car door. My father erupted, screaming and pacing on the gravel driveway. His face was purple and his arms were flailing. My mother was speaking softly and calmly. Finally he yelled something and threw himself back inside a silver car and immediately took off. I didn't know whose car it was.

When my mother and I walked back inside, there were three gold-wrapped presents sitting on the kitchen table, marked "To William, from Santa Claus."

Building C, Apartment #3, Hunter's Glenn Court was my mother's address. The apartment was decorated with the mandatory festive material. There was a Christmas tree covered with silver tinsel and randomly placed red balls. A tiny glass angel was set at the top. That was the only ornament familiar to me. The apartment itself was hypermodern. The kitchen had slabs of phony marble, a microwave oven designed to fit inside the wall, and a stainless steel refrigerator. The living room was spacious, with sliding glass doors on one wall that looked out onto ten thousand other identical apartment buildings. It was a two-bedroom. I'd been there a few times before when my mother first moved in, but I hadn't ever lived there.

Harris was pretty much of a prick. That was clear from the get-go. Everything about him was pompous: the way he sat on the couch with one hand placed on his stomach, his fingers diving a few inches into his pants; the way he rattled the ice around in his scotch; the way he waited for my mother to feed him. His hair was white and he was wearing a brown sweater. It all made him look far too old for my mother.

He was watching a football game.

"Hey, William," he said, standing up. "It's a pleasure to meet you. Your mom tells me you're a hell of a guy."

We shook hands. He was sure to give me a good, sturdy shake. His hand was clean like a surgeon's. I could feel the grooves in his skin.

"Who's playing?" I asked. He told me. I couldn't have given

a shit. I thought about telling him to get out of my house but it wasn't mine. He had pictures up on the wall, pictures of people I didn't know. There was a zebra-skin rug on the floor. That had to be his.

"I didn't know you two were living together," I said.

My mother gave me a look. She had an apron on. I couldn't believe it. I didn't know what game she was playing. I'd never seen her wearing an apron in my life.

"Harris moved in two weeks ago," she said. "I told you that."

She introduced me to Harris's parents. They were preposterously old. I wanted to leave. I wondered when I was going to be able to stand still.

"Do we have any chips and salsa?" I asked my mother.

"Don't spoil your dinner," she said.

I found the chips and took them out anyway. I set them down on the table and went to the fridge to get the salsa. My mother took the chips away and removed the salsa from my hand.

"I'm making a nice dinner," she said. "Come on, it's no fun if we're all not starving." I couldn't believe the charade that was happening around me. I hoped everyone was impressed.

My mother sat me down in front of the football game with Harris and his parents. We all exchanged courteous smiles. Harris pointed out his favorite advertisements when they appeared on the screen.

One of them was a Miller Lite ad with about fifteen blazing chicks in G-string bikinis.

"Take a gander at that, William. Can you believe that?" he said.

I nodded. He leaned over to me, so that his mother couldn't hear him speak.

"Just remember this, William: for every sweet, little honey out there, there's some guy who's sick to death of balling her."

I nodded. My heart was pounding. I was worried my thoughts were being projected out loud.

"I'm sorry my girlfriend, Sarah, couldn't be here today. She really wanted to come," I said. I felt like lying.

"We didn't expect anyone at all, so it's a pleasure just to have you," said Harris.

I excused myself and went to the bathroom.

By the time we sat down for dinner, I had gone to the can about eighteen times and was convinced I had to go again. It wasn't that I was drinking profusely or anything. I just kept having the sensation I was going to wet my pants.

My mother chirped away maniacally as she passed around the food, desperate to avoid any silence. Harris's father was so quiet I was sure he was deaf. His mother was clearly a drunk. In between slurring her words and repeating herself, she was hawking my mother. She nibbled the food slowly, with displeasure. Harris kept scooting back his chair and leaving the table to check the score.

"William just turned twenty-one," announced my mother.

"When Harris was twenty-one, he was out tomcatting around every night," said his mother. "He had more young ladies than he could shake a stick at."

Harris winked at me.

"I'd love to be twenty-one again. You enjoying it?" he asked.

"It's fantastic," I said.

"I think it's an important year," said my mother. "And not just because of drinking and things like that."

"Something makes me think that William's birthday wasn't the first time he had a drink," said Harris.

"No, I don't think so either," my mother said, smiling, "but I've always thought that life moves in sevens: fourteen is puberty; twenty-one is the start of adulthood; twenty-eight is real adulthood; thirty-five is middle age. It always seems to me that big changes occur in my life every seven years." She took a long pause. "I can't think of any examples right now but I'm positive that it does." She laughed.

"I think life moves in elevens," said Harris's mother. "Christ died at thirty-three, you know."

"That's true, isn't it?" asked my mother.

"Yes, it is," she answered. The old woman was nodding so ferociously I thought she might fall out of her chair.

"I wonder what the score is," said Harris, getting up.

"Why don't we just bring the TV in here and turn the sound down?" my mother suggested.

"You hate television, Mom," I said.

"I know, but Harris won't be happy unless he knows the score at all times." She said this as if it were the most charming characteristic anyone could possibly imagine.

"Harris has always been a real sports nut," said his mother.

"I couldn't give a fuck," I said. It came out before I realized how it sounded. My mother looked at me. She wasn't angry; she just took me in for the first time all afternoon. I'd blown her cover.

My mother continued leading the table in a conversation. I excused myself to take another leak. I thought I might walk back out naked.

I loved my mother. I even kind of wanted to really talk with her. Christmas depressed her, too. Harris shouldn't be allowed to stand in the kitchen and carve the turkey like he was Elvis Presley. I knew he was thinking smarmy thoughts about my mother. The whole situation repulsed me and it always had. We were advertisements of ourselves. The meal was an advertisement of Christmas. I thought we should all be eating in bikinis. I missed my father, but that seemed absurd. I didn't know him well enough to miss him. I tried to simply miss Sarah; it was easier than dealing with all the other crap swimming around in my head.

When I walked out of the bathroom, I realized I'd forgotten to take a piss. Before I could go back in, my mother snuck over.

"Are you all right?" she asked.

"I want to call my dad," I said. "Do you have his number?"

"Let me go get it," she said. "Do you want to call him right now?"

"Yeah, I think so."

"All right." She moved to find it. I was surprised she wasn't angry. I knew I was behaving like an eight-year-old.

"I'm a little old for this, huh?" I said, trailing behind her.

She left me in her bedroom with the telephone number. I didn't know what I was going to say to him. I wondered if I was finally going insane. My mother dated a guy once who was hospitalized for insanity. She lived with him when I graduated high school. He was cool. I'd been in a funk the day of my graduation because I thought that I should've been given a family heirloom as a present — only we didn't have any. So this guy took me on a walk and gave me his oldest pair of blue jeans.

"It's not an heirloom, I know," he said, "but they are old. They're from the fifties, I think. I've had 'em forever."

"Thanks," I said, holding them in my hands.

"This is the only advice I have for you." We were standing on a tree-lined street outside our old house. Some parts of New Jersey are undeniably beautiful. "Your whole life people are going to ask you to be weak — they'll practically beg you — but all anybody ever wants from you, no matter what they say, is for you to be strong. You remember that."

I liked that man. I wished my mother was still dating him. Of course, he ended up in a mental hospital and I have no idea what happened to his jeans.

My mother's bedroom was loaded with trinkets from the past. Items I remembered from other homes we'd had. There was an old quilt on the bed that her grandmother had stitched. There were pictures of her father in World War II. None of Harris's shit was in there yet. I wondered if he had condoms tucked in the bedside table. The thought made me sick. I felt dizzy; it was as if my body were filled with helium and might blow away. I thought I could see trees through the walls. I thought I could see the ink where the Fort Worth area code was written bleeding through the paper and dripping out onto the floor. I called him. I just did it.

She answered. Lindy, my stepmother.

"Hey, Lindy, it's Will. Merry Christmas."

"Oh, my," she said. "How are you? Where are you?"

"I'm in New Jersey."

"Hey, Vince, William is on the phone!" she hollered. "Are you having a fun Christmas?"

"Yeah, real fun," I said. For the first time in weeks I wasn't nervous. I wasn't playing with the telephone cord or pacing, or anything. I was numb.

"Good, well, here's Vince."

"See ya," I said.

"Hey there, William," he said. He had a pleasant, soft southern accent. I wanted to tell him everything that had ever happened to me.

"Howdy," was all I said.

"What's going on? Where are you?" he asked. He sounded in good spirits.

"New Jersey," I said again.

"Oh," he said. There was a tremendous amount of noise happening around him. It was the sound of kids experimenting with new toys.

"Merry Christmas," I said. I turned off my mother's lamp. The light was scalding my eyes.

"Well, Merry Christmas to you, too."

"You watching the football game?" I asked, standing in the dark.

"Nah, are you?"

"Nah. . . . Cowboys are doin' pretty good this year, though, huh?" I didn't know if they were or not.

"It's real exciting around here," he said.

"Do you remember Super Bowl twelve?" I asked him. I didn't know why I'd brought this up.

"Uh . . . yeah. . . . Who was that? Cowboys and the Steelers?"

"No, it was the Broncos. Cowboys and the Broncos. We won that year."

"Oh, sure. That was something else."

"It was Tony Dorsett's rookie year. You remember him?"

"Of course," he said. "He's from Wylie, Texas."

Even in the dark my eyes burned. I needed to take out my contacts. I heard my father muffle the phone and tell someone to please quiet down.

"So how ya been?" he asked.

"I fell in love with this girl but she broke up with me," I said.

"Oh, yeah, I've had that happen."

"You have?" I asked. I sat down on the bed.

"Oh, sure. I remember the first time I got up the guts to ask a girl to one of our high school dances. She said that she couldn't come 'cause she'd be away on vacation with her folks, but sure enough she showed up at that dance with ol' Bobby Miller."

"That must have been a drag," I said.

"Yeah. Took me years to work up the nerve to ask out another girl." He let out a short chuckle.

"Well, this girl's name was Sarah. She kind of broke my heart, I think."

"That'll happen," he said.

"Did my mom break your heart?" I asked.

There was a long pause.

"Oh, I don't know. That was a long time ago," he said.

"Well, you got over it, huh?"

"Yeah, sure did," he said softly.

"How you been?"

"Oh, we're having big grins around here," he said, his voice becoming louder. He was pleased to have the subject changed. "Same old shenanigans. David and Hillary are practically real people now. They've grown up like a couple of weeds. You'd like them. Lindy's pulling her hair out with Laura Lye and Katie. They're only two and three." He paused for a moment. "You've never met any of the kids, have you?"

"No," I said.

"David's a hell of a football player."

"Is he a Cowboys fan?" I asked.

"The biggest," my father said. All of a sudden I hated the Dallas Cowboys.

"Look, Dad, I gotta go. I just wanted to wish you a Merry Christmas." I stood back up. I dug my fingers into my eyes trying to pinch out the contacts.

"Look, William, I'm glad you called. We've been meaning to give you a call, and I'm sorry I haven't done it." He was trying to be nice and it made me feel awful.

"I'd like it if we kept in more touch," he went on. "Every family's got its foibles, and, uh . . . I know we've got ours, but, boy, I want to tell you that I think it'd be great if we could talk more. You're welcome here anytime."

I got my contacts out and flicked them onto the floor. I wanted to get off the phone.

"Sometimes late at night I sneak downstairs and watch David's football games on the VCR."

"You tape his games?" I asked.

"It's my favorite thing to do. Eat a couple cookies and watch his games again. And it can't help but occur to me all the things we missed."

I stood motionless in the dark of my mother's bedroom.

"I just wanted to wish you a Merry Christmas," I said. "That's all."

"All right. Well, I'm sure glad you called," he said.

I set down the receiver gently. That was the first time we'd spoken in seven years.

I walked outside. I must've seemed drunk. I tripped three times on my way out. I couldn't see much of anything without my contacts. The cold air felt good. I could breathe again. The sun was setting. The light wasn't anything spectacular; it was just the ordinary sun dropping down. It left all the barren trees in silhouette against the dim sky. The snow was falling more heavily now. A few inches had accumulated on the ground. I heard my mother's steps crunching behind me.

"How did it go?" she asked. She didn't have a jacket on either. Her arms were wrapped tightly around her.

"It went all right," I said.

We stood in silence. She was waiting for me to say more. I looked out across the bleak New Jersey landscape and the apartment complex surrounding us.

"I loved that stupid girl so much, Mom," I said.

A mound of snow was collecting on top of my mother's head. It must've been on mine as well.

"I fell in love with your father because he told a funny joke," she said.

"That doesn't always work," I said. My voice was hollow.

"My point is only that it's all pretty arbitrary," she said, lightly stomping her feet. "Sometimes, William, you just have to decide not to go crazy. Sometimes all we have is our decisions."

My mother was a high school dropout. Martin Luther King Jr. was assassinated her junior year, and the day after it happened, her history teacher made a wisecrack about it. She closed her book, picked up her purse, walked up to the front of the class, and said, "You make me want to puke." She left school that day, drove down to Houston, where my father was going to college, and never returned. I always liked that about her.

My mother reached over and handed me an envelope wrapped with a lavender ribbon.

"Look at this," she said with her teeth chattering. "I found it a couple months ago. It's a present. I'm going back indoors." She shook her hair out and scampered back inside.

I opened the envelope. It contained two sheets of paper covered with my own handwriting. I held them close to my face so I could read them. The snow falling made a soft patter on the pages.

William Harding age 7

The Cowboy

The cowboy rides
Through desert by desert
Traveling by horses
He gets dirty
Like a rag buried in the sand
And he dies full of age
and bullets.

The Hat

A hat is shaped in lots
 of different ways.

A big bump in the middle
And flat on the sides
And nothing like a jacket.

The Hottest State

Fort Worth is the hottest state I know
My dad lives there
My grandma too
Most every grandparent
except a few.
I like it there
Boy is it hot.

Tarzan kissing a girl:
    baby, baby, baby.

I folded the two sheets of paper and inserted them into my
back pocket. The snow on top of my head was melting down
my forehead. For some reason, I wasn't cold at all.

TWENTY

"It's kind of like this," Decker said: "You wake up in the middle of the night and you're dying for a glass of milk. So you stumble out of bed, stub your toe in the darkness, scream with pain, and limp your way to the refrigerator. You open it up and the light is brilliant. You're saved. Then you fold back the paper container, open up the milk, take a deep breath, and put it to your lips. Only — *yhrch!* — the milk is spoiled. Sure, you're bummed. You fold the thing closed and put it back in the fridge. It's dark again. But as you're making your way to your lonely old bed, you think to yourself, Wait a minute, maybe that milk wasn't so bad. And I am still thirsty? So you do an about-face and go back to the fridge. The light warms you up again. You take a sip and, yup, it's still spoiled. That, to me, is the fitting metaphor for most every relationship I've ever been in."

Decker was sitting on a box and endlessly bullshitting with me as I packed up my junk. I was moving. It was early April and my hair was hanging down past my shoulders. I hadn't shaved in months and was sporting a skimpy-looking beard.

Sarah had called me that morning. I didn't even recognize

her voice. If she had called one day later I would've missed her entirely. She was working at a preschool in Brooklyn now and invited me to visit her on her lunch break. I accepted and was planning to head out there the next day.

I wondered what she was going to say. I had a secret day-dream that perhaps she was pregnant, and that was the real reason we broke up. I'd show up out in Brooklyn and Sarah'd be fat like a balloon with our child. Her mother would be there as well, pointing a knotty, stern finger at me, saying, "When are you going to start taking responsibility for this child?" I would scream, "Right now!" and that would be that. I knew the scenario was a little far-fetched but I liked it.

We packed everything away except the stereo. We listened to Bob Dylan and the Band's *Before the Flood* at full throttle, tossing a baseball back and forth. Music sounds superb in an empty apartment.

Decker was getting prepared for a six-month writing fel-lowship over in England. He wasn't too keen on the British but was looking forward to the time away.

"I wish I was more repressed," Decker said, giving the ball a toss.

"Why's that?" I asked.

"I just think I'd have a better time," he said. "Did I tell you my new resolutions?"

"Nope." I threw the ball back to him.

"I want to try to never waste energy degrading someone else. Also, I want to try not to see life as a competition. If I can do those two things, as well as keep myself from being checked into an alcoholic rehabilitation center, then I figure I'll be A-OK."

"I just want to make it through tomorrow," I said. There's something very calming about throwing around a baseball.

"Whatcha worried about?" he asked. "Sarah called you, right? Just go in there without an agenda and listen to what she has to say."

"What do you think is going to happen to the two of us?" I asked.

"What d'you mean — you and me?"

I nodded my head yes.

"Like, in general?" he asked.

I nodded again.

"Pretty soon we'll both probably get busy with one thing or another, and then before you know it, the whole ride'll be over." He threw the ball back to me.

Finally we packed up the stereo and started carrying it downstairs. I had two neighbors that I'd hardly spoken to in the year that I'd lived there. They were a fragile old couple that I'd only seen occasionally lurking in the shadows behind their door. We kept very different hours. The woman was the most splendid-looking elderly lady I'd ever seen, with icy, delicate features and long, flowing white hair. I offered to help her carry her groceries once, but she was scared to death of me.

As I was exiting my apartment with several of my stereo components in my arms, I saw the old man poke his head out his door. She was right behind him, trying to listen.

"Hello there," said the old man. He wasn't much over five feet tall. "Are you moving out?"

"Yes, I am," I said in my most polite tone.

"Well, I wish you much luck," he said.

"Thank you."

"I can't say we'll miss you," he stated simply. His voice sounded very educated.

"Oh, yeah? Why is that?" I asked. Decker filed in behind me, carrying more of the stereo.

"To phrase it as pleasantly as possible," he said, "you make a hell of a racket."

"Jeez, sir, you really should've said something," I said. Decker was starting to laugh.

"That's what my wife always said, but I don't believe in complaining," he stated firmly and closed the door. I rethought the past year's events, this time inserting an image of two ancient, frightened people peering over their blankets, listening to the tornado that lived next door.

TWENTY-ONE

I took the bus out to Williamsburg. I liked Brooklyn. It looked to me as I imagine Manhattan looked in the fifties. There are many small shops with people standing out front smoking, drinking, and talking. I had Sarah's address written on a ratty scrap of paper.

The preschool was in the bottom of a church — a little, brick, square building with a flat, green lawn in front and the East River behind. The front doors were glass with children's drawings taped across them. An older woman sat in the front office. She told me Sarah had taken the kids out to the park but that they'd be back in a jiffy.

I was wildly relieved. I was feeling short of breath and I was glad for the extra time. There was a poster board up on the wall with about twenty kids' names written on it and rows of gold and silver stars next to each one. I wanted a star. I wanted fifty stars. I wondered what it took to get one. I peeked my head in the classroom. The lights were off but I could see tiny, little chairs delicately placed underneath miniature tables. There were cardboard pictures of frogs and tigers.

I decided to wait outside so I could see when she was coming and so that maybe I could smoke a cigarette. I thought better of the cigarette, though, because I didn't want her to come prancing over the hill all pristine with the delightful children and me to be sitting there in some cloud of smoke and mildew. I wished I had dressed better. I wished I had gotten some sleep. There was this little bench outside the school that I sat on for a long while, trying not to be anxious. I didn't want to be foolish and anticipate anything unrealistic.

The first thing I saw was her hair. It had grown much longer and her curls made long, black ringlets that almost looked like braids — except that a few of them were sticking straight up. She made me smile. She was wearing a brown dress with brown tights. I couldn't hear her, but she seemed to be reprimanding the kids for not staying in line, madly pointing everywhere.

They all came up over the lawn walking in twos, holding hands. It was difficult to look straight at Sarah's face. I wasn't sure I wanted her to see me. When the first couple of kids walked passed my bench and through the glass doors, I heard one say to the other, "I know. That happens to me ALL THE TIME." He couldn't have been more than six.

I thought that was hilarious. I wanted to say, "*What*, kid? What happens to you ALL THE TIME?"

Sarah didn't see me until she was almost at the doors. I was grinning from watching the children.

"Oh, hi," she said, and walked right by me.

I sat there blinking.

She popped her head back out.

"I'm sorry. Come on in. I'm very nervous."

"Yeah. Me, too," I said and followed her inside.

Sarah had a Band-Aid across the bridge of her nose and several others covering her arms.

"What happened to you?" I asked.

"What do you mean?" She was bending down and tying the laces of her shoes.

"What's with your face?" I asked.

"Oh, yeah," she said, scratching her head with her pinkie finger and then brushing her hair back. "I got chicken pox a few weeks ago."

I thought that was funny.

"What?" she asked.

"I don't know. I'm sorry. It just struck me as kind of humorous."

"Well, it isn't. It's dreadful and I'm very embarrassed." We were standing in front of the classroom beside the poster with all the stars and finding it very difficult to look at one another.

"I'm not contagious," she said sharply.

"That's all right. I've already had 'em anyway."

She was more shaky than I was. Neither one of us knew what to do with our hands.

"Come on in. I'll introduce you to the class," she said, moving away.

"Oh, no, that's okay, I'll wait for you outside. I look kind of scary." My hair was shaggy and I should've shaved, but I thought that if I didn't, I'd have an easier time just being myself.

"They don't care. Come on." She walked into the classroom. I crept in after her. The room was different with the kids in it; it seemed to be painted a thousand colors, and everything appeared to be bouncing.

"Class, this is William," Sarah announced. "William, this is my class — the best nappers in Brooklyn." There was a smattering of agreement.

"William is an actor. He was in a movie."

I wished she hadn't said that. I thought it made me sound cheap.

"No, he wasn't," said one of the boys.

"Sanger, do I ever lie?" Sarah asked.

Sanger and I both thought about that for a minute.

"No," said Sanger.

"All right, then. William is an actor and he's been in a movie. Isn't that neat?"

I was still thinking about the lie question. Maybe I'd take Sanger aside later and tell him she doesn't exactly lie, but that he's not crazy; she isn't entirely trustworthy either.

Sanger came up to me. He was a brown-haired kid with a New York Jets T-shirt on.

"Were you really in a movie?" he asked me suspiciously.

"Yeah, I was."

"My dad's a mechanic. He fixes cars," Sanger said challengingly.

"That's cool," I said.

"We have a Corvette."

"No kidding?" I asked.

"I'm gonna be a football player," he said, daring me to defy him.

"That's what I want to be, too," I said.

Sarah was on the other side of the room, fiddling with some girl.

"Now, Elizabeth, what did you do with your dress?" she

asked as she untucked the little girl's dress from her underwear.

I walked over to Sarah and stood near her. I wasn't sure
what I was supposed to be doing with myself.

"They're going to lie down for a nap soon, and then we can
talk, okay?" Sarah was on her knees with the little girl climb-
ing on her head.

I took a step back, patted my pockets to make sure I still
had my cigarettes, and perused the kids. They were going
bonkers. I couldn't imagine any of them napping.

"It's painting time now. Do you feel like painting?" she
looked up at me hopefully.

"Sure," I said. It was turning into a very odd afternoon.
Sarah proceeded to seat all the kids down at the four diminu-
tive tables and gave each table one color. Sanger and I each
chose the blue table.

Sarah orchestrated the room gracefully. She stopped the
crying, cleaned up the spilled paint, and provided the proper
encouragement to all. It was clear to me that she'd make
someone a hell of a mother.

I felt a slight tug at my pants. I looked down and there was
a little girl with straight, jet-black hair, giant blue eyes, and a
red-floral dress gazing up at me.

"Yes?" I said.

"I have to go," she said.

"Go where?" I asked.

She tugged at her crotch.

"Oh, all right. Ah . . . hey, Sarah. This one has to go to the
bathroom," I called out across the room.

Sarah was sitting down helping some fat kid with her
drawing.

"That's Amanda. Would you take her?" she asked.

"Your name is Amanda?" I looked back down at the kid.

"Uh-huh." She nodded her head.

"Do you know where the bathroom is?"

"Of course," she said.

"Let's make it happen."

She grabbed my finger and led me into the bathroom. It was narrow inside but she insisted I come all the way in. Then she closed the door. I was terrified. I didn't think I had ever really watched a girl take a leak before.

She pulled down her underwear. I turned around. She sat down on the toilet and did her business. When she finished, she asked me for some toilet paper. I handed it to her, happy that was all I was needed for.

"Thank you," she said. She opened the door and hauled ass back to her table. I was fuckin' exhausted.

I sat down next to Sanger, thinking that maybe we had some kind of connection. I helped him paint a blue football field, complete with hash marks and two end zones. When we were finished, he was emphatically proud of it and rushed over, holding it out for Sarah.

Still using only the color blue, and then stealing a bit of black for the hair, I made a finger painting of Sarah. I took it over and showed it to her.

"That's nice," she said.

"It's for you." I'd written her name boldly in sloppy handwriting across the top of the page.

"Thanks. I have about a hundred of these," she said.

Sarah moved to the center of the room and clapped her hands five times fast.

"Okay, now, everyone. Time to put the paints away and get ready for our nap. But before we nap we'll have a story. So the sooner we clean up, the sooner we get to hear the story." There were general sounds of disgruntlement throughout the room.

"And guess what?" Sarah went on, in an attempt to subvert the unhappiness. "We have a special reader. William will read the story this afternoon." I could feel the children's eyes all scrutinizing my appearance.

"No, no," I said. "I'm really not much of a reader."

"Everyone who comes to visit has to do the reading," she said smiling.

I had a sudden flash that this whole afternoon was some bizarre ritual she put all her ex-boyfriends through.

The kids tidied up the room, and in no time at all the entire class was assembled Indian-style on a brown rug in front of a stool. Sarah handed me several books and said to pick one.

"So, what? I just sit here and read it?" I asked, pointing at the stool.

"Yes, but talk about the pictures. They like the pictures."

"Is this a good story?" I asked, picking one out.

"They're all good," she said.

I sat down on the stool, with a big, square, colorful book in my hands and stared at the kids. I cleaned my glasses with my shirt. They were all squirming and playing with one another's hair. One kid had her head stuffed inside a bookshelf. Sarah was looking at me from the back of the classroom, with her Band-Aids across her face, signaling for me to start.

"All right, you guys. Here we go. Y'all better quiet down or I won't be able to read this thing." For some reason I was speaking with a slight southern accent. "This book here is called *Father Bear Comes Home.*" I took a deep breath. "And this story is called 'Little Bear and Owl.' Do y'all know this one?" I looked out at the sea of small faces.

Amanda gave me a quiet "yes" but most of the other kids were just glaring.

"Well, let's just hope that it's good." I held the book up and pointed to the illustrations.

"See, here we got a picture of, I guess, Little Bear, and it looks like he's checking out a portrait of his old man there on the table." I pointed to the detail in the drawing.

"And his mother comes over and talks to him." I was startled that I actually had their attention. I was sure one of them would start complaining any moment.

I braced myself and began reading.

" 'Little Bear,' said Mother Bear, 'can you be my fisherman?'

" 'Yes, I can,' said Little Bear."

I smiled at Sarah, letting her know that everything was going to run smoothly. She motioned with her hands for me to keep showing the pictures.

"Ah, yes. See, everyone? This here is Little Bear's mom. You can tell she's his mom 'cause she's got an apron on and all." I thought Sarah might get a laugh out of this last observation, but she simply sat patiently waiting for me to continue.

I turned the page.

" 'Will you go down to the river? Will you catch a fish for us?' said Mother Bear.

" 'Yes, I will,' said Little Bear."

I kept on reading and showing the pictures. The story followed Little Bear down to a river, where he meets his buddy,

Owl, and proceeds to catch a puny little fish. Little Bear gets all bent out of shape that his fish is too skimpy and talks about how he wishes he could be like his dad and catch big octopuses. I liked this story.

I turned the page.

" 'I know what,' said Little Bear. 'We can make-believe. I will be Father Bear. You can be you, and we are fishing.' "

Little Bear and Owl then begin pretending to reel in a whale and a giant octopus. I looked up at Sarah. It was so good to see her again.

Amanda interrupted me and asked, "Are you sad?"

"No, no," I said, looking down at her.

"Why are you crying?" she asked.

"I'm not crying, Amanda." I didn't think that I was. I flipped the page fast and my heart started racing. I noticed that my glasses were misting. I could barely breathe.

"Look, here. Look at Little Bear now," I went on. "He's imagining he's all dressed up in his dad's clothes and he's got — What's that on his fishing line?" I asked, pointing down at the drawing of Little Bear's imaginary octopus.

"Hey, mister," said Sanger. "It looks like you're crying."

"Well, I'm not." I tried to laugh but that didn't help. I looked up at Sarah. She had her chin resting on her hand, and her green eyes were searing through me. She gave me the tiniest of smiles.

I turned the page.

Mother Bear had come along and discovered the two pretending. Little Bear defended himself.

" 'You will see. When I am as big as Father Bear, I will catch a real octopus.' "

When I said that, my voice dropped an octave. I forced myself to keep reading.

"Owl said, 'Little Bear fishes very well.'
" 'Oh, yes,' said Mother Bear. 'He fishes very well indeed.
He is a real fisherman, just like his father.' "
That was the end of the story.
"Oh, Christ," I said. I had to look down.
"It's not a sad story," said Sanger.
"Yeah, I know, man, but it's a good one, don't you think?"
"The next one is better," he said.
"That's all for now," proclaimed Sarah. "Time to turn off the lights and prove to William that we are indeed the best nappers in Brooklyn." The kids all started moaning again. I thought maybe I heard some complaints regarding my reading but it didn't last for long. Slowly everyone pulled out their mats, positioned themselves near their friends, and lay down for a nap.

Amanda wanted me to hold her hand while she tried to fall asleep, but so did a couple of other kids. I felt very popular.

Amanda insisted that I come with her. She escorted me to her mat and I lay down beside her.

Before she fell asleep, Amanda whispered, "I think that story is sad, too. I think all stories are sad."

I closed my eyes and tears silently rolled down my face. With the lights off again, the room was like it was when I first arrived. It was quiet and all of the colors seemed subdued. I was exhausted.

When the children were down, the older woman returned and gave Sarah the cue that it was all right for us to leave.

We started sneaking out the door. Sanger stood up and walked over to me.

"Are you going to be here when I wake up?" he asked.

"I don't think so," said Sarah. "Hurry up now, get on back to sleep."

"My dad doesn't think the Jets are going to win the Super Bowl, but I do," he said.

"They've got as good a shot as any," I told him.

Sanger stuck out his hand for me to shake it. His fingers were small and I could feel his developing bones. He turned around and strutted back to his mat.

Sarah and I slipped outside to the back of the church. There was a small promenade by the East River with several people meandering about on their lunch hour. We walked together for a few minutes. The wind was blowing along the river in powerful gusts. Sarah was forced to walk with both hands firmly holding down the hem of her skirt.

"I have an hour," she said. "Do you want to talk?"

I thought about that for a minute.

"You know what? I think I'm going to go home," I said.

"Are you mad?" she asked.

"No, I'm not mad. I'm just really tired and I'm not so sure there's much to say." I wasn't mad.

"William," she said. Her hair was leaping in the wind above her head. "I just wanted you to come out and see where I work. It always seemed to me that you had a very false notion of who I was. I'm not any fantastic thing, you know? I'm just a preschool teacher."

I started laughing.

"What?" she said. "What are you laughing about?"

I shook my head and said, "Nothing."

She looked at me the way she always did, as if she didn't believe a word I said.

In the trees above us the wind was rustling the leaves into a frenzy. Sarah said something I couldn't hear.

"I said, 'You handled the kids very well,'" she repeated. "Thank you."

"It was no problem," I said.

"What?" she said. Sarah stopped walking.

"I enjoyed it," I said, raising my voice.

I leaned on the railing and looked down at the water. I'd always heard about what a garbage-filled cesspool the East River was, but from Brooklyn it looks glorious.

It was difficult to actually say good-bye. A hug or a handshake would've been silly, so I kissed her on the cheek. Her skin was soft and for a second I remembered how she smelled and tasted. I didn't want to dwell on that.

At one point I turned and watched her walk away. She was still holding down her skirt with both hands, and her hair was dancing above her. I could see one of her Band-Aids glued to her elbow.

I turned around and started up the slope toward home. The wind felt fresh against my face. I thought of my favorite thing to do when I was Sanger's age. I would go out on the street and stroll along through the people, thinking of myself as an orphan. That always felt good. I did that again, there by the East River.

ACKNOWLEDGMENTS

First off I would like to thank Jennifer Rudolph Walsh for drinking beer, talking slowly, and agreeing, against her better judgment, to represent an actor. I would also like to extend my gratitude to Austin Pendleton for his inspirational dresswear and his outlaw theories; to Nicole Burdette; to Patrick Powers, the Irish Saint Poet Hero of New Jersey; to Captain Patrick Powers Jr. and Miss Heather Powers the First; to the Niagras for giving it all, all the time; to Helen Childress for staying up late and listening; to Richard Linklater — no cute phrases for you — just thanks; to Fred Leebron for being an ornery son-of-a-bitch who for some reason kept digging this story out of my drawer; to the spirit and all the individuals of the Malaparte Theater Company; to Danielle Beach; to Susan Dineen; to Dr. Anthony Zito; to Bryan Lourd. To Jason, Josh, Bob, and Frank — my friends. And to Jonathan Marc Sherman, the underground inspiration to all of Manhattan — ya ya the clown — mastermind of Jimmy Bonaparte, night owl, crusader for the morally righteous and decadent, I thank you for introducing me to all that I know.

Jordan Pavlin I cannot thank enough.

Special thanks go out to my father, James Hawke, for being so accepting of all the baggage that accompanies a son who aspires to a life in the arts. And finally, I thank my mother, Leslie Green Hawke: Lost Princess of Abilene, Queen of the River, and Patron Saint of my favorite bird, the lark.